CR

Adventure New Zealand: Beneath the Totaras

A Sequel To
Whims, Wits, and Whiskers

Sieglinde C. Othmer

Illustrations By Clare Rosean and Julia Othmer

Music by James T. Lundie and Julia Othmer

authorHOUSE®

AuthorHouse™
1663 Liberty Drive
Bloomington, IN 47403
www.authorhouse.com
Phone: 1 (800) 839-8640

Published by AuthorHouse 11/02/2017

ISBN: 978-1-5462-1278-2 (sc)
ISBN: 978-1-5462-1277-5 (hc)
ISBN: 978-1-5462-1276-8 (e)

Library of Congress Control Number: 2017915854

Print information available on the last page.

This book is printed on acid-free paper.

A Tale About

Adaptability
Ambition
Compassion
Courage
Emotional Control
Hospitality
Imagination
Manners
Respect
Trust
War
Will Power
And how apologies and forgiveness can heal the heart.

Also by Sieglinde C. Othmer PhD:

Berlin und die Verbreitung des Naturrechts in Europa. Kultur- und sozialgeschichtliche Studien zu Jean Barbeyracs Pufendorf-Übersetzungen und eine Analyse seiner Leserschaft. Berlin Walter de Gruyter & Co. 1970

The Clinical Interview Using DSM-III-R. Washington DC American Psychiatric Press 1989 (with Ekkehard Othmer)

Psychiatric Diagnostic Interview, Revised (PDI-R) Manual and Administration Booklet. Los Angeles CA Western Psychological Services (WPS) 1989 (with Ekkehard Othmer, Elizabeth C. Penick, Barbara J. Powell and Marsha Read)

Life on a Roller Coaster. Coping with ups and downs of mood disorders. New York The Berkley Total Health Series, Berkley Books 1991 (with Ekkehard Othmer)

The Clinical Interview Using DSM-IV. Vol. 1: Fundamentals, Vol. 2: The Difficult Patient. Washington DC American Psychiatric Press 1994 (with Ekkehard Othmer)

The Clinical Interview Using DSM-IV-TR. Vol. 1: Fundamentals, Vol. 2: The Difficult Patient. Washington DC American Psychiatric Publishing 2002 (with Ekkehard Othmer)

The "Clinical Interview" books have been translated into Italian, Spanish, Portuguese, Korean and Farsi.

Whims, Wits, and Whiskers—A Californian Pet Tale. IUniverse, Inc. Bloomington 2012

To

Ekkehard
Konstantin and Deborah
Philipp and Jennifer
Julia and James

With Lots of Love

"You are a child of the universe, no less
than the trees and the stars.
You have the right to be here."
Desiderata

⊚⊚ Table of Contents ⊚⊚

Characters

The Cousins:
   Mr. Guinness—Labrador Retriever/Pit bull, alpha dog
   Lexi—Shih Tzu, companion to Rosie
   Rosie—Terrier, companion to Lexi
   Bailey—Labrador Retriever, partner to George
   George—Beagle/Basset Hound, partner to Bailey
   Miles—Black cat, buddy to Cosmo
   Cosmo—Tabby cat, buddy to Miles
Aunt Jetta—Blue Heeler
Chiara—Condor
Hank, Harry and Helen—Hummingbirds

The New Zealanders:
   Mitch—Tri-colored Sheltie, leader of the sheep herding dogs
   Leo—Red barn cat in charge of pest control
   Angus—Ram, rusty brown, companion to Aliya
   Aliya—Ewe, rose colored, companion to Angus
   Colored sheep
   White sheep
   Pigs
   Peter, Paula and Paul—Blue Penguins
   Sam—Stoat, leader of the stoat clan
   Rock Hopper Penguins
   Albatrosses

Images ⊚⊘ ⊘⊚

By Clare Rosean

By Julia Othmer

Music

Track 1: Believe
Track 2: Get Together

Music is available at www.sieglindeothmer.com

Acknowledgements

I would like to thank my husband for letting me do my thing; my children, Konstantin, Philipp and Julia, for rescuing and caring for the characters in my story; Tammy Parsons and Darlene Carpenter for introducing me to Mitch, their dog; Dorrit Bender for having Leo, the cat, and for hosting her delightful Swedish club dinners; Janet Samuelson for her consistent kindness; Patricia Hamarstrom Williams for her indomitable, irresistible and full swing laughter; Edward O. Wilson for developing the concept of biophilia; Lauren Bamber for her editorial attention to detail; Claire Rosean for her inimitable illustrations; James T. Lundie for bringing the songs to life; Cheryl Ferguson for teaching me how to be dramatic; and the staff at AuthorHouse for their professionalism.

Finally, I would like to thank my daughter Julia for her eye-opening edits and for inspiring me with her authenticity, her tenacity, and her dedication to her music. Without her, this book would not be.

◎◎ A Letter to My Adult Reader ◎◎

Dear Reader,

It was early morning one February, during a family trip on the other side of the world. The ship we were on sailed from the choppy Tasman Sea into the serenity of Milford Sound. Milford Sound is part of the Fiordland National Park on the New Zealand South Island, not too far from Antarctica.

The vertical scale of the mountains in Milford Sound boggled my mind. Sheer rock and lush rain forests rose straight out of the deep green waters to a height of 3,900 feet. Waterfalls cascaded down to seals that warbled on the rocks below. Fog rose from the water. The 2,000 passengers on the deck of our ship fell silent, in awe of the spectacle. We were in the midst of a world heritage site. Rudyard Kipling called it the eighth wonder of the world. This is what Captain Cook saw when he came here in 1769. So pristine, so dense, so mysterious these woods looked that maybe, in their thicket, the moa, believed extinct, has survived. And if not the giant moa, then maybe a little one.

While there, I learned about New Zealand's preservation efforts for their endangered species. One afternoon, on a cruise ship stop, we took a car ride from Christ Church to a nature sanctuary on Banks Peninsula. It seemed like the end of civilization. We continued in a four-wheeler that bumped us through a wilderness of dunes to a point on a hill, where we left the buggy and hiked down. Along a bay swelling with giant kelp and frolicking baby seals, the nature guide took us to a viewing station. An encased platform made of wood, with slits to peek through, called for halt! Privacy! Keep out! For ten years no human had walked on the beach below. Through a telescope, we observed an emperor penguin emerge from the water, upright with importance, waddle across the sand upward into tufts of tall grass on the dune and disappear. We focused the scope on the backside of a little blue penguin, sitting on the nest in a stone crevice minding the egg. To see such purity of nature was magical.

I fell in love with this land.

The experience of New Zealand impacted me so that at home, I started spinning my tale. As I wove it together, more than New Zealand's fauna and flora found their way into my story. It became a vessel for all that I love.

I love to travel. As a college student, I became an au-pair in Paris and studied at the Sorbonne. I visited the Louvre once a week, and sang with a student choir in the Cathedral of Rouen. The next summer I took trains to see Spain. Alone. This was unheard of at the time, as many señoras and señoritas told me. I spent the nights in convents, dining on bread and milk with the nuns. I saw Madrid, Burgos, Avila and Andalusia. When I visited Granada to experience the splendor of La Alhambra I found it rather provincial, after witnessing the glory of Versailles. After I married, I immigrated to the United States and raised a family. There was more travel. With my husband and kids, I had the good fortune to see more of Europe, Asia, Africa, the Americas, Australia and New Zealand.

I love nature; to be outside is the best. I like watering, weeding, and walking. Even in the rain. Even in the cold. As the Icelandic saying goes, there is no bad weather, only bad clothing. I love animals. When ladybugs wander into my house, I help them get back outside. Watching a pair of foxes with their three cubs play on my deck one April morning gave me a delight that lingered for weeks, just like the comfort you get from your cat or dog giving you a kiss. I also love plants. I'm fascinated by the mystery of a seed—I enjoy watching two tiny round basil leaves break the soil.

I love to study. I am fascinated to learn that, when sensing danger to their existence, plants communicate above and below ground. When peril presents, they produce odors called volatile organic compounds. And below ground, soil fungi in addition to common mycelial networks, which act like fiber optic cables, let roots communicate. I find that utterly amazing.

What I'm saying is I find nature inspiring. Observing and interacting with it fills me with wonder, happiness and inner peace.

I also love research. At the University of Hamburg I took a class on the history of Human Rights—the stimulus for my Ph.D. thesis. It describes (in German) how, in Berlin, at the end of the 17th century, a Huguenot, expelled from France, translated his favorite Latin legal text into French. This very translation spread the popularity of the Human Rights idea in Europe in the 18th century. The ultimate consequence were the American and French Revolutions. When I found out that Rights were extended to non-humans, namely the great apes, and that New Zealand was first on earth to do that in 1999, I had to include that in my story.

With all this love going on, the academic in me scrounged around and investigated the concept. Where English has only one word for it, the ancient Greeks have six. They are:

Eros—sexual love, with loss of control (which the Greeks feared).

Storge—love in the family between parents and children.

Agape—charitable love, or the love of God.

Pragma—the longstanding love of older couples, with patience and tolerance.

Philantia—the love of the self. And finally ...

Philia—friendship, fondness, a tendency for deep affection.

Further reading led to the work of Edward O. Wilson who coined the word biophilia, combining philia with 'bios,' which in Greek means 'physical life'. That word sums up what I wrapped into my tale—the love for life on this planet.

And one more thing. I also love music. Appreciation for music is in my DNA. As it happened, my singer/songwriter daughter Julia and her producer husband James Lundie composed tunes to go with my fable. Their music is on my website. My characters love to sing along, and I hope you will too.

Sieglinde C. Othmer PHD
Kansas City, Missouri 2017

⊙⊙ Family Map ⊙⊙

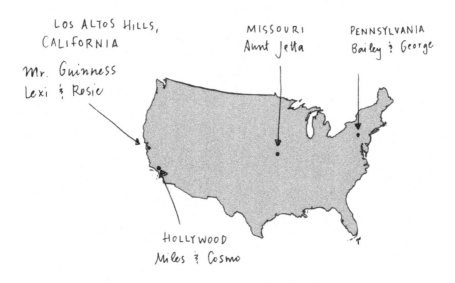

LOS ALTOS HILLS,
CALIFORNIA

Mr. Guinness
Lexi & Rosie

MISSOURI
Aunt Jetta

PENNSYLVANIA
Bailey & George

HOLLYWOOD
Miles & Cosmo

⊘⊘ Chapter 1: News ⊘⊘

"Rosie! Wake up! Rosie! Hurry!" Lexi pressed her face against the living room window and shook her blond mane. "Come here! That giant bird is back! The bald-headed one with the angel wings. Look! Guinny is talking to her."

Rosie leapt up from her morning nap and rushed to the window. "Ahh!" she gasped. "It's Condor. I've been thinking about her all summer."

Lexi looked at Rosie inquisitively. "You have? Why didn't you say so?"

"I tried, Lexi, but you were too busy."

"I'm never too busy for you, Rosie."

"Except when you binge-watch TV, which you do all the time."

Lexi bit her lip and edged closer to Rosie as they stared out the window. Lexi, a seven pound, champagne-colored powder puff Shih Tzu, and Rosie, a woolly, gray Tibetan terrier mix, lived with the aforementioned Guinny, a black Labrador-pit bull, in Los Altos Hills, California, in a house on a hill overlooking the San Francisco North Bay.

"What are they saying?" Lexi wondered. "I can't hear anything."

"Me neither." Rosie focused on the scene outside. "Can you read lips?"

"No. Can you?" Lexi asked in wonderment.

"No."

The two held their breath, straining to hear.

Rosie broke the silence. "Look! See that? Guinny is smiling! Must be good news."

"Last time Condor was here she promised us adventure. Remember, Rosie?"

"Of course, I remember. How could I forget?" Rosie pranced on the spot.

"Do you remember her name?"

Rosie stood still and her eyes widened. "Hmm … wait! Did she ever say?" Rosie stared at Lexi and then barked over her shoulder. "George! Bailey! Wake up!"

George, a stately beagle/basset hound, lumbered from the closet. "Can't a dog sleep in this house? Just got here yesterday. We are on vacation!" He snorted. "What's so important down there?" Yawning, he bumped into his buddy, Bailey, a yellow Labrador, who nudged him right back. George peeked out the window and started barking. Bailey raised her head.

"We're not entirely sure *what's* going on, but *something* definitely is," reported Rosie.

Lexi trembled with excitement. "Miles and Cosmo! Come see!"

Snoozing on the tapestry couch, Miles, a sleek black cat, and Cosmo, a tabby, opened their eyes halfway. They had also arrived the day before from their home in Hollywood and were still recovering from the six hour journey. They had come to Northern California to celebrate Thanksgiving.

It was the beginning of Thanksgiving week. Everyone looked forward to the holiday traditions of long daily walks for the dogs and lots of naps for the cats culminating in a feast of turkey with crispy skin, stuffing with gravy, garlic mashed potatoes, yams with butter, a green bean casserole, cranberries steeped in orange juice, and vanilla ice cream on apple cinnamon pie.

"*Bonjour,*" Miles yawned.

"*Ouf!*" Cosmo blinked. "It's too early to get up." The cats rarely felt the need to hurry out of bed.

"You'll want to see *this!*" Rosie insisted. "*Now!*"

Gingerly, the two best friends jumped off the sofa. Caution served the cats well. They angled their way over to join their dog cousins at the window. They took one look outside and recoiled.

"Woah!" Cosmo gasped. "That beast could eat us for breakfast."

"*La vache!*" Miles raised his brow, but did not lose his cool. "*Excusez-moi*! Is this for real? *Qui est-ce?*"

Lexi turned to face the cats. "That's Condor. Last time she was here, she told us to not be afraid. I know she looks scary but she has kind eyes and a really melodious voice."

Cosmo demurred. "I'll stay inside for now."

3

Announcement

*****

Outside, on the far edge of the patio deck, Mr. Guinness (Guinny for short) faced an immense, black-feathered bird, more than twice his size, whose ebony bulk was crowned with a bald orange head.

Condor had first visited them in the spring. She had learned about their artistic family troupe of five dogs—Mr. Guinness, Rosie, Lexi, George and Bailey—and two cats—Miles and Cosmo, and their smashingly successful performance in the Midwestern town of Parkville. Upon hearing of their performance, Condor had come to Mr. Guinness with a proposition: if the cousins desired to do more shows, she and her fleet would fly them south to tour the Americas. As artistic director of the troupe, Mr. Guinness had longed to speak with Condor all summer and autumn, eager to follow up on her proposal. And now, the timing for another show was perfect: all his cousins were here.

So that morning, when Mr. Guinness saw Condor swoop into the backyard, his heart jumped. He took a deep breath, got up quietly so as not to interrupt everyone's morning slumber, and tiptoed through the doggie door. Then he dashed to the patio's edge.

"Welcome!" he said, a bit out of breath.

"Hello," Condor replied softly. "Good to see you, Mr. Guinness."

"The pleasure is mine," he responded. "I was hoping you would return."

Condor came right to the point. "I trust you know why I'm here." She fluffed her feathers.

Mr. Guinness sat up straight. "It's time for the tour of the Americas?"

"It's time to take you on *a* tour. And yes, while the original plan was for Central and South America," she aired her wings, "the situation has changed."

"Changed? How?" Mr. Guinness's voice was a pitch higher than he intended. The words escaped him quickly.

"You and your troupe could make a grand difference in another part of the world."

"A grand difference..." Mr. Guinness's voice trailed off. His eyes opened wide. His ears perked. His front paws pressed the ground. "In another part of the world?"

"Are you interested?" Condor bowed her head to gaze gently into Mr. Guinness's eyes.

"Yes." He did not hesitate for one second. As an entrepreneur, he was always open to new opportunities. As an artistic director, he would do anything to set up another show. That was the dream of his life. He wanted to perform for the world! "Where would we be going, exactly?"

"Across the Pacific Ocean." She paused for a moment, drawing out the suspense. "Across the equator."

"The equator!" Mr. Guinness swallowed. "West and south! What location do you have in mind?"

"New Zealand."

"New Zealand? That's near Australia!" He knew quite a lot of geography. At corporate headquarters he had studied world maps and their different time zone clocks.

"Yes." Condor smiled.

Mr. Guinness loved her idea. Now he would have to figure out the logistics. His first concern was his troupe's well-being. Where would they stay? What would they eat? Would they find a performance venue?

As if she could read his mind, Condor spoke up. "The albatrosses are my liaisons in New Zealand. They survey both land and water and know what's going on. They told me about a special pig farmer. He is renowned for his kindness. He keeps his animals rosy clean, gives them fresh water every day and mixes their slop with organic carrots and bananas. He also loves music and thinks animals love music too. And it is true. They do. His pigs thrive on listening to the symphonies he plays from speakers in the rafters of the barn. Mostly Mozart. He runs a pig paradise. His farm would be an ideal place for you to stay."

Mr. Guinness was all ears.

"The pig farmer's wife is special too," Condor continued. "You see, in New Zealand it is common practice to kill all sheep who are not purely white at birth, because they are not considered valuable. Well, *she* believes *all* sheep are precious and deserve a good life. So she rescues the variously hued lambs. All over the island, she collects these unwanted creatures, takes them to the farm and raises them. She spins their wool to knit children's hats. The animals on their farm would be your hosts. New Zealand's hospitality is known to warm the heart."

Mr. Guinness relaxed his neck muscles. "That sounds amazing! Is there a place to have a show? What about a stage?"

Condor smiled. "New Zealand has a myriad of options. It has hillsides that form natural amphitheaters, vast sandy beaches with dunes and wide meadows as green as the emerald sea. Possibilities for staging a show are everywhere."

Mr. Guinness felt his tummy getting warm. Optimism welled up within him. He wagged his tail. "And an audience?"

"Many sheep live on that farm," Condor said. "They, too, listen to Mozart, when the pig barn doors are open. They will welcome a show. And they could spread the word. Over a million sheep graze in New Zealand."

"A million sheep? Wow! Do you have any other recommendations or advice?" Mr. Guinness asked.

"Let your intuition guide you. But if I may make a suggestion— local talent delights any audience. Our friends, the albatrosses, are fabulous dancers. Perhaps you could ask them to join you on stage."

"Dancing albatrosses? I'm so curious." Mr. Guinness reminded himself to stay professional and focused. "What is the timeline for this project?"

"I have a squadron available now." She spread her massive wings to check the wind direction. The breeze tickled her feathers.

"I would like to consult with my troupe and see if they want to go."

"You will find a great sense of pride if you pursue this mission." She closed one eye in an exaggerated wink and turned her face to the sky.

"Mission?" Mr. Guinness's ears perked forward. "Wait! You said mission. What do you mean by that?"

Condor turned her head. "First things first. Find out if you all want to go. Then connect with the hummingbirds. They are apprised of the situation and will let me know what you decide," Condor said, churning the air with her wings.

"Condor! One last thing!" Mr. Guinness raised his voice to make sure she heard him. "You never told me your name."

"My name is Chiara. My friends call me Chiara Mia. I do hope to see you soon." She lifted off majestically.

Mr. Guinness watched her disappear above the horizon. He closed his eyes. His heart brimmed with joy. Another show! International travel! A friendly place to stay! He pumped his paw, expanded his chest and—head high—sniffed the air. He raced back and forth along the length of the deck feeling alive with possibility. He sensed with excitement that there was something in his future that he could not yet fathom. He inhaled and exhaled three times. Then he stretched—head forward, tail straight— upward facing dog yoga pose, and held it extra-long. Then legs back and head down for downward facing dog pose. Yoga helped him focus.

Lexi and Rosie began barking at the window, impatient for his return. With a bounce in his step, he headed toward the house and entered through the doggie door. Immediately, Lexi and Rosie swarmed him.

"What did you talk about?" Lexi jingled her collar.

"Oh, tell us! Guinny, tell us! What was going on down there?" Rosie hopped up and down.

"It's so early in the day," George grumbled. "It better be good!"

Bailey was right at his side, her tail wagging expectantly.

The cats stared, then blinked and sneezed, faking nonchalance.

Mr. Guinness sat down in front of his cousins—chest strong, ears up—and looked them in the eye, one by one, thrilled by the dogs' curiosity. "I have news—big news!"

Lexi and Rosie rubbed their sides against each other. Bailey and George touched shoulders. The cats perambulated languidly, gently, on velvety paws, undulating their tails in slow motion.

"First, let me get everyone up to date." Mr. Guinness turned to Miles and Cosmo, George and Bailey. "After you went home last spring, Condor visited us, raved about our work in the Midwest and proposed to take us on tour."

"On tour?" Bailey hated to interrupt but could not help herself.

The cats inched closer.

"What's the news!?" Rosie demanded impatiently.

"The trip is on, but not as we had planned. We will not be going south along the coast of the Americas, not to the place where our hummingbirds spend the winter. Condor wants us to go someplace else."

Rosie grinned. "Well, I don't care where we go, as long as we go, and we do it together."

"It was so much fun last time," Lexi cooed.

"Is it Africa?" George bellowed, dancing excitedly on his short stout legs. "I want to go to Africa!"

Bailey smiled.

The cats fixed their eyes on Mr. Guinness.

Miles took in a deep breath. "*Parbleu!*" he whispered to Cosmo. "Is a world tour finally within our reach?"

"You saw that big beast of a bird!" Cosmo hissed back. "Clambering up on top of that? That carnivore is the top of the food chain. Consider!" Slowly, he pushed a loose pile of playing cards off the edge of the coffee table.

"*Mon ami,* Cosmo! *As artistes* we must be flexible and collaborate with all kinds of characters," Miles said calmly. "We must dare. For art's sake."

Cosmo closed his eyes, leaned back and stayed silent. His tail switched back and forth in agitation.

"We all would like to perform again," Bailey said. "What about this new destination?"

"I will tell you what I know," Mr. Guinness said. "Condor wants us to go to New Zealand."

"Where in the world is that?" Rosie barked.

"It is across the Pacific Ocean," he paused to let the news sink in.

"Across the ocean? How big is the ocean?" Lexi asked.

Rosie barked. "The Pacific Ocean is very big. I know that."

"That just means it's a longer flight, right?" Bailey asked.

"Well, yes." Mr. Guinness appreciated Bailey's realism. "And conditions for a show are ideal in New Zealand. We'd have accommodations, a stage and an audience, pretty much guaranteed. I do believe this is a once-in-a-lifetime chance." He inhaled deeply and exhaled. "I think we should go. I'm in. Are you with me?"

Bailey threw adoring glances at Mr. Guinness; she admired his leadership. "I'm in, Guinny. I would like to go." In actuality, she would support any plan he came up with.

George wrinkled his brow. He frowned and walked backwards, away from the group. "New Zealand?" he grumbled. "Newshmeeland!" He raised his voice. "Where's that? No one's ever heard of it. I want to go to Africa! I've always said that!" He

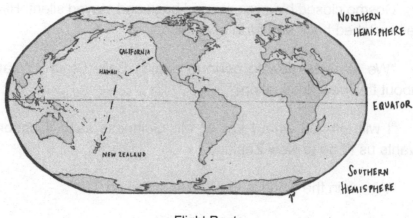

Flight Route

barked and took off through the doggie door, down the hill, past the shed, and toward the fence, howling all the way.

Bailey turned to the group. "Please, excuse me. I think it's best I go speak with him." She darted after him. George was her priority right now; a massive temper tantrum was coming and she needed to stop it before it got out of hand.

Down by the fence, George started to dig, spritzing dirt everywhere. "I'm leaving!" he roared.

"Where will you go?" Bailey bobbed her head to avoid the clumps of grass and flying pebbles George sent her way.

"To Africa, of course!"

"George!" Bailey closed her eyes, shook her head and sat down. "That's not the way to get to Africa! Digging won't get you there!"

"It will get me somewhere," bellowed George.

"Yes. Somewhere like the doghouse! George! With these cousins of ours, with our performance, there's a good chance we will get to Africa someday just not yet. And not with an attitude like this."

George did not listen. He labored at his dig, hot-tempered, spraying earth, gravel and stones, pushing his hulk deeper and deeper under the fence. Bailey stared at him and realized he was too worked up. He would have to tire himself out. She wondered what was happening with the others. She ran up the hill to recruit help. No one was on the patio, so she went inside.

In the living room, Mr. Guinness had his paws full. Rosie was jumping up and down in front of him. She was hounding him with questions. "Is New Zealand by Tibet?" she asked. "Can we see the Dalai Lama?"

Mr. Guinness smiled. "You always think big, Rosie. I love you for that. But Tibet does not line up as a stopover on the way to New Zealand."

"Well, I want to see the world," Rosie said. "All of it. I want adventure. I'm in. When do we leave? We have to get ready, don't we? Don't we?" She looked around for Lexi. She saw a champagne-colored paw poking out from under the couch. Rosie hunkered down. "Lexi! What's wrong?"

Flat on her belly, Lexi blinked at Rosie. Then she turned her head, focused her attention on her leg and started to scratch. "What about Thanksgiving? What about our humans, our Master and Missus? Someone needs to stay with them," Lexi winced. "They need me here. You can do without me." She bit her lip, rubbed her face and scooted further back underneath the sofa.

"Master and Missus go on trips without us and they are okay. Isn't that the same thing?" Rosie asked with her ears perked forward.

"Well... maybe."

"What do you mean, 'maybe'? It's exactly the same!" Rosie insisted.

"But, Rosie..."

"Yes?"

Lexi turned away and bit her toes. "I'm scared to be in a strange new place."

"Don't be a sissy. Remember our fun in Parkville?"

"Yes," Lexi whimpered.

"Were you comfortable there?"

"Yes." Lexi blinked. She stopped shaking.

"It was a strange new place, but once you got there, you loved it. And," continued Rosie, "you played the role of a lion on stage. You showed such gumption."

"I did?" Lexi raised her head and tilted it to the side. "I tried really hard. But that was just an act."

Rosie grinned. "Even if it *was* an act, I know you have courage."

Lexi gave Rosie an uncertain look. "I don't know. I'm overwhelmed. This is too much."

"It won't be any fun to go without you," insisted Rosie.

As she continued to soothe Lexi, Mr. Guinness turned to the cats. The moment George began his fuss, they had retreated to the living room corner. Cosmo was curled up into a tight ball, his head in his belly. But Miles stepped forward and raised both front paws in victory pose.

"*Monsieur Guinness! Monsieur le Directeur!* So long have I waited for this day. *Merveilleux!* Our show will go on," Miles was on a roll. "A call to perform again with our cousins! Imagine! Another chance to fulfill our dream! *Superbe! Splendide! Magnifique!*"

Mr. Guinness smiled. "So glad you are on board, Miles. I know that together, we can handle any challenge. We will make our show bigger and better than before. I have faith in us." The two hi-fived.

There was a small meow from the corner. Miles turned to Cosmo. "You want to do this, *n'est-ce-pas?* We may have a few kinks to smooth out... *peut-être* ... but we want to do it... definitely... that's why we came to Los Altos Hills, *n'est-ce pas?*"

Cosmo uncurled from his fetal position and splayed out on the parquet floor. "Another show? *Oui!*" He raised his head and peeked at Miles. "But flying across the ocean? *Non!*" He winced. His stomach was in knots. "*Jamais!*"

"You have flown before," Miles reminded him.

"Yes," Cosmo nodded. "B-u-t there was a plane with sides and windows and doors. To travel on a monster bird over open water?" Cosmo shook his head. "Following the coast line going south is one thing—we can land any time if something goes wrong. But crossing the sea? We could drown. I'm not going. Not me. You are beyond nuts."

Miles moved closer and licked Cosmo's face. "*Mon cher ami*, there is no reason to freak out."

Cosmo stared at his buddy. "Yes! There is!!!" Not one French word came to his mind. He was too upset.

Miles sighed heavily. "Cosmo! You love being an *artiste*, *oui* or *non*?" It sounded more like a statement than a question.

"*Oui*," Cosmo agreed.

"Our life goal, my friend, is to create, to perform, to entertain. We want to move our audiences with dance and song. *Oui* or *non*?"

"*Oui*." Cosmo stared at his front paws, his brow knitted, ears down.

"We must have conviction." Miles nudged him on the nose. "This is a way to live our dream." Miles stared into Cosmo's eyes.

Cosmo stared back. "I need time to think." He bee-lined to the exit.

Miles called after him. "I'll be here if you need me, Cosmo. We will find a way. Nothing is impossible for us cats," he shouted. "*Rien!*"

Cosmo did not listen. He was out the doggie door and on his way to the top branches of the olive tree, where he could be alone.

Rosie, Bailey, Miles and Mr. Guinness convened in the center of the living room.

"How are we all doing?" Mr. Guinness breathed calmly.

"I'm in, but Lexi is not." Rosie rocked from left to right, moving so quickly that her ears flopped. "She is crying under the couch. She's afraid to leave home."

"Let George vent his frustrations," Bailey said, "but I'm in. I'm all in."

"Me too, *mes amis*," Miles affirmed. "Though Cosmo needs a moment to himself to fathom the possibilities."

"Okay, we are divided 4 to 3," said Mr. Guinness. "Let's take a moment, let everyone process a bit and then regroup." As he considered the domestic drama, he was not disheartened. He hoped Cosmo could be convinced that the reward was worth the risk. He believed George would recover from his tantrum and that Lexi would find her courage.

Miles spoke up. "Cousins! My fellow *artistes*!" He positioned himself in the middle of the living room, one foot forward, one paw extended, like an orator before a crowd. He raised his voice so Lexi could hear him from under the couch.

Rosie stood still in awe.

"We must inspire one another. We must encourage one another to be creative, to take risks, and embrace the unexpected."

Lexi came out from under the couch to watch.

"Whatever fear we may have right now, that fear pales—I repeat, it *pales* in comparison to the tragedy of a life without art. *Quelle horreur!*"

Mr. Guinness winked at Miles. "Bravo!" he said.

Bailey thumped her tail.

Miles radiated passion. "*Mes amis! Merci.*"

"Miles," Mr. Guinness asked, "will you please join me outside for a moment?"

"*Bien sûr. A tête-à-tête* in the fresh air? Cool off? Gain perspective under the open sky?" To Rosie, Lexi, and Bailey he said, "*Excusez-nous!*" Miles nodded to Guinny. "Shall we go now?"

Hummingbirds— *Selasphorus rufus*

Just as Mr. Guinness was about to say yes, a commotion interrupted him. It came from outside the window. Tiny beaks tapped the glass. Teensy bodies fluttered, whirled, and twirled. The hummingbirds had returned.

Chapter 2: Help

"**L**ook!" Rosie nudged Mr. Guinness in the butt. With her ebony nose, she pointed to the trio of birds hovering outside the patio window. "It's Hank, Harry and Helen. They must have come to fill up on nectar. Our lavender pentas are still blooming."

Starcluster Pentas—
Pentas lanceolata

Three sets of beaded black eyes looked through the glass.

"Hello, everyone!" Hummingbird Hank chirped through the window pane. "Yes, your pentas are delicious, but we came to fill you in on the mission."

"I was hoping you would show up." Mr. Guinness was thrilled they had arrived. He was anxious to know what they knew about Condor's proposal. "Cousins! Shall we join the birds outside? I would certainly like to hear what they have to say." Mr. Guinness pushed through the doggie door. Bailey and Rosie followed. As did Miles.

"*Monsieur* Guinny, please excuse me," he said, "I will check on Cosmo." Miles was determined to calm Cosmo's fears and convince him to join the tour. There had to be a way to win him over.

Miles joined Cosmo in the heights of the olive tree. Crouching down close to him and watching the scene unfold beneath them was a good start. And it was excellent theatre.

Mr. Guinness sat down with Rosie and Bailey below the bustling hummingbirds who turned triple summersaults above them. Talking to birds seemed to be the theme of the day—first to Condor, the largest bird on Earth, and now to the hummingbirds, among the world's smallest. Down the hill, beyond the shed, George was still indulging in his fit.

"How has he not tired himself out yet?" Rosie whispered to Bailey.

"When it comes to digging, he has stamina." Bailey sighed. "We all cope differently when things don't go our way."

"What's up with him down there?" Hank chirped. He and his charm of birds darted back and forth, up and down. "I sense all is not well."

"There has been an unexpected change in plans. That is how George is dealing with it." Mr. Guinness raised his voice. "Miles and Cosmo are thinking it through up there in the olive tree. Condor Chiara has proposed to take us to New Zealand. She said you would have more information for us. Is New Zealand even a part of your migrations?"

"Never," Hummingbird Helen said. "It lies beyond the Pacific. We do not cross that kind of water."

"But Condor said to speak with you about a mission, a mission to New Zealand." Mr. Guinness was eager to hear.

"Yes! That's why we are here," said Hummingbird Harry. "Worldwide, we keep up with the latest. We have heard that New Zealand is beautiful. It's a land of lush mountains, spectacular waterfalls, geysers, hot springs, fjords, and volcanoes. But as beautiful as New Zealand is, there is serious trouble."

"What's going on?" asked Mr. Guinness.

"Gruesome things." Helen grimaced.

"Strong intervention is needed," added Hank.

Rosie interrupted. "Intervention for what?"

"For the kiwis, the birds without wings," Harry said. "They are facing extinction."

"Extinction?!" Rosie was aghast. "Like getting snuffed out?"

"They are in danger of being killed off. Forever."

"Forever?" Bailey sat back on her haunches, her eyes as big as saucers.

"How horrible!" Mr. Guinness gasped.

"Your mission is to help keep that species alive," announced Harry. As if to emphasize his words, a swarm of hummingbirds appeared.

"Us? That's a very tall order." Mr. Guinness barked with excitement. "How can we help?"

"Your performance in Parkville brought everyone together," declared Hank. "Maybe you can bring some harmony to New Zealand as well."

Mr. Guinness was fascinated. "What do you propose?"

"Have you ever heard of a benefit show?" asked Helen.

"Benefit? What do you mean *benefit*?"

"Benefit," interjected Rosie, "means a good thing." She hopped up and down. "When you do someone a favor, they benefit."

"Yes, Rosie, thank you. But what is *a benefit show*?"

"A benefit," Hank said, "is a performance put on for a special purpose. You raise awareness about a vital issue, such as the kiwi's struggle to survive."

"A show with a special purpose!" Mr. Guinness caught on. He loved new ideas. He knew the universe was abundant with them if he kept an open mind.

Harry hovered around the dogs' heads. "You could not only do a great show, you also serve an important cause. That could take your performance to a whole new level."

"I love a challenge...," Mr. Guinness hesitated, "but I need my group's consensus. Some of us are working out a few personal concerns right now."

"Can we help with that?" asked Helen.

"Yes, please." Mr. Guinness felt they could use all the help they could get. "George is throwing a fit because he wants to go to Africa."

"Our Cosmo has a fear of flying," Bailey added.

"And," continued Mr. Guinness, "Lexi is concerned about leaving home. We have our work cut out for us, all right. But where there is a will, there is a way."

"Let us handle George," Helen announced. She raised her beak high. The entire swarm of hummingbirds focused on her. She nodded over to where George was digging. The charm swooped up as one unit and zipped downhill. Bailey ran after them.

Two feet under, George had hit a layer of rock. He was trying to dig around it—thrusting his nose harder and harder. The hole was getting larger by the minute, earth spritzing, pebbles spewing, clumps flying. The excavation was already large enough for his bulky body to fit in and he showed no sign of stopping.

The hummingbirds knew what to do: divert his attention. United they swooped in close hovering mere inches from his head. He could not keep digging without causing a bird collision. Frustrated, George stopped and looked up at the creatures circling his head.

"Leave me alone!" He snapped at them, but they were too quick. "Buzz off! Get out of my face!" he bellowed.

"George!" Bailey's voice rang out above the whirring of the birds' wings. "Listen! Hummingbird Helen wants to speak with you!"

"Bailey!" George shouted. "Help dig! To Africa!"

"No, George! We need to talk!"

He ignored her and, at a frenetic pace, resumed his activity. "Africa or nothing!"

The hummingbirds switched gears. Upon Hank's command, they went on the attack. Hummingbirds versus hound—a black cloud of intensely whirling bodies, crowded right around George's head, in his face, on his nose, like a massive swarm of very large bees. Up they surged, out of reach, and down they came, their wings beating faster than any other bird's on earth: 200 beats per second, five milliseconds per beat, quicker than George could ever snap.

He shook his head and body to free himself, but to no avail. The hummingbirds kept pouncing—assault and rebound. On top of all this, they gleefully dropped poop so tiny and ethereal that it glistened in the sun like diamonds. Even though some evaporated before landing on him, the massive glare stunned George.

"Fine!" he huffed. "Okay! I've stopped. Now what?"

"Remember the last time we were here, George?" Bailey chimed in, "Digging up a mess got us into trouble. We had to fill in more holes than I care to remember."

"Hey, George!" yelled Hank. "Where are you trying to go anyway?"

"Africa." George breathed heavy.

"Why Africa?"

"I want to hunt wildebeests."

"Oh! Are they about to leave Africa?" Hank smiled. "What's the hurry? New Zealand sounds just as exciting."

"George! What could be awesome about New Zealand?" Bailey hoped for a good outcome. "Think of the possibilities! There may be other exotic animals—kangaroos, koalas, unicorns? It's not Africa, but it will be an adventure for sure."

George stared at Bailey. He hated to disappoint her. He gazed up at the hundreds of hummingbirds circling him, focused only on him. He sat down in his dug-out, threw up his head and treated everyone to a long, loud, ear-boggling howl.

"Stunning!" Harry whistled. "You must share your gift with the world! The world must hear your songs!"

"Did you say 'stunning'?" George shouted. "Yes! I am a stunning hound! I stunned an audience before. By golly, I will stun them again! Let's go to New Zealand!" He stepped away from the fresh pile of dirt, puffing, snorting, and smiling.

"You must be thirsty," Bailey sighed with relief. "Come up to the house. Let's have a refreshment."

George *was* hot *and* thirsty *and* his hip hurt. He allowed Bailey to usher him up the hill. The hummingbirds escorted them, twirling in somersaults. Mr. Guinness and Rosie waited on the patio, delighted to see them come up.

*****

From their perch in the olive tree, the cats had watched the hummingbirds corral George. Their ears twitched to catch every word. "Looks like George is on board. Guinny is high-fiving him. *Merveilleux!*" Miles turned to Cosmo. "Isn't that marvelous, Cosmo?"

Cosmo scratched his ear. "I don't know."

"Oh, won't you join us on the journey, *mon ami*?" Miles licked Cosmo's back. "It wouldn't be the same without you. *Jamais.*"

"Flying across the ocean?" Cosmo gulped. "I'm terrified."

"Of what?" Miles asked, even though he knew.

"That we crash into the water!" Cosmo wailed. "I can't deal with it."

Miles looked him in the eye. *"Mon cher ami..."*

"I freak out when I fly. If I fell asleep at the start of the trip and didn't wake up until we arrived on the other side... maybe I could handle it."

"Ah oui! Naturellement! We will find a way to soothe your anxiety," Miles reassured him. "There is aromatherapy. Lavender calms the nerves. We'll dry it and take it with us as medicine. I'll rub peppermint oil on the bottom of your paws for sweet dreams."

"Will that work?"

"Oui. Certainement. I will bring sleepy time tea, a sleeping mask, and ear plugs to minimize the wind noise."

"Really?" Cosmo perked up. "I did bring my sleeping socks. As if I knew I might need them." Cosmo gave Miles a grateful look. "Thank you for not making fun of me." He loved his buddy. He wanted to be with him always, and he wanted so badly to be an artist on stage once more.

"I know you feel like this is scary." Miles continued, "But *not* going is as scary to me. Sitting at home doing nothing freaks me out. Even though it feels safe, not taking chances is dangerous for our well-being. Inactivity wastes talent and numbs the joy of living. What kind of life is it, if we don't dare?"

Cosmo blinked. "I don't want to waste my talent."

"*Non!*" Miles agreed.

"I would regret it, if I didn't try. I would never forgive myself." Cosmo teared up. "You are right, Miles. Not trying is worse than failing."

"*Monsieur!* You are a tom-cat!" Miles put his paw around Cosmo's shoulder. "We might even have fun."

Cosmo lifted an eyebrow. "Fun?"

"Do we ever NOT have some kind of fun?" asked Miles.

Cosmo shook his head.

"So shall we?"

Cosmo nodded. "*Oui.*"

Paw by paw, with Miles in the lead, the cats climbed down. Once the olive tree was cat-free, the hummingbirds settled into its branches, everyone except Helen. She flew up to the house and hovered over Mr. Guinness, whispering in his ear. Mr. Guinness grinned, nodded and went to meet the cats.

"Cosmo, my cousin," Mr. Guinness said, "I hope you are alright."

Cosmo inhaled and exhaled. "Working on it, Guinny. I'm a bit nervous. Be patient with me, *s'il vous plaît.*"

Mr. Guinness smiled. "Of course, my friend. Hummingbird Helen just told me that if you decide to go, Condor Chiara will have an extra squadron of condors flying underneath us, as a security net of sorts. Does that help you feel better?"

"Yes," Cosmo sighed with relief. "That would be really groovy."

A wide grin spread over Mr. Guinness's face.

"So it is decided?" Miles was excited to get the show on the road. "When do we leave?"

"Well," Mr. Guinness turned his face toward the house, "we are not *all* decided yet."

"Lexi?" Cosmo asked.

"Yes," Mr. Guinness said. "I'll find her."

*****

The living room seemed empty.

"Lexi!" Mr. Guinness called out.

No answer. Rosie nodded toward the couch.

"Lexi, my dear!" Mr. Guinness dropped to his belly and scooted forward so he could see her eye-to-eye. "What's bothering you?"

Lexi did not stir.

Mr. Guinness nudged her gently with his nose. "I wish you'd come with us. We love your company. It could never be the same without you, little lion."

Lexi lifted her head. Her collar jingled just a bit. "What about Thanksgiving?" she whispered. She poked out her bottom lip and pouted.

"What about it?" Mr. Guinness asked.

Lexi hesitated. "Where will *you* be on Thanksgiving?"

"In New Zealand."

"And Rosie?"

"In New Zealand."

"And Miles and Cosmo?"

"In New Zealand."

"And Bailey?"

"She will be in New Zealand, too."

"Even George?"

"Yes, even George. If *you* come, we will *all* be in New Zealand: the seven of us *together.*"

Lexi scooched forward and stuck her head out from under the couch. "I do want to be with you on Thanksgiving. Wherever you will be, even in New Zealand."

Mr. Guinness gave her a kiss on the nose. "I'm proud of you. Let's tell the others."

They went outside to the patio, where the cousins eagerly awaited. The hummingbirds descended from the olive tree.

Sounding like rain, they buzzed with excitement. Their little voices rose in a melodious chorus. "Everyone on the same vibe? Are we in harmony?"

Mr. Guinness spoke. "Yes! I believe we are. Thank you for your help. We will start planning immediately."

Hummingbird Hank approved. "Your mission is urgent. You need to depart sooner rather than later. We will report back to Chiara and then head south for the winter. As a parting memento, may we offer you a gift? Something of a musical nature?"

"Yes, please!" The cousins were delighted.

"Would you like to hear our travel song?" Hank asked. "It has our mantra in it."

"A mantra? What's that?" Lexi asked.

"A mantra is a word or a phrase that you repeat."

"Like a chorus?" Lexi asked.

"Yes, like a chorus. When you say or sing it, it inspires you. It lifts you up and gives you confidence." Hummingbird Helen continued, "a mantra can dispel anxiety and generate courage in the face of uncertainty. On our long trips, it energizes us and our young ones."

"We sing it as we fly. It has a terrific effect," Helen said.

"Really?" Mr. Guinness's curiosity was piqued. He wondered if a mantra would be helpful for his troupe too. "May we hear it?"

"Sing it!" chanted Rosie. "Sing it!"

"Yes!" Lexi yipped agreement, dancing on her hind paws.

As their conductor, Hank hovered in front of the charm and raised his beak. The hummingbirds cleared their tiny throats. With a signal from Hank, they began to sing.

"YOU GOTTA BELIEVE
YOU GOTTA BELIEVE
BREATHE IT IN
LET IT GO
BREATHE IT IN
LET IT GO
BREATHE IT IN
LET IT GO
YOU GOTTA BELIEVE
YOU GOTTA BELIEVE."

"Is there more?" asked Cosmo. "Your flights, you say, are long?"

"Oh yes," Helen chirped. "We have many verses. We sing about the beautiful world we fly over and all its possibilities, about what we make of them and ourselves. Our song teaches our young to expect the unknown and to persevere even if they feel scared. Here is a sample."

Hank raised his beak again. On cue, the charm began to sing.

"You know the world keeps on rolling on by.
It is so beautiful from up in the sky.
There is so much to see,
So many places to be.
Where do I really want to go?
What do I really want to know?

I listen to what my heart tells me
And go with the flow.

YOU GOTTA BELIEVE
YOU GOTTA BELIEVE

And if the way ahead isn't clear,
Or if you're feeling maybe some kind of fear,
That's alright.
It is just letting you know
That there is something here that you just don't know.
You don't need to fear what is unknown—oh no.
Trying something new is how you grow.
Listen to what your heart is telling you
And you just go with the flow.

YOU GOTTA BELIEVE
YOU GOTTA BELIEVE

Cause you can walk a million miles in irrelevant directions
If you don't know what you're looking for.
But take it from me!
Then you can wake up in a world of possibility.
Believe that you can see the world is everything you want it
to be!

BREATHE IT IN
LET IT GO
BREATHE IT IN
LET IT GO
BREATHE IT IN
LET IT GO
YOU GOTTA BELIEVE
YOU GOTTA BELIEVE."

The cousins kept still in stunned silence. In a grand gesture, Mr. Guinness raised his front legs over his head, held the pose for a moment and put his paws together to applaud. "Bravo!" he shouted and his cousins cheered. "Thank you! We should learn this song for our new show. Would you give us permission to use it?" He winked at them. "We'll give you credit, of course."

"Our pleasure," Hank, Harry and Helen said in unison. "We wish you luck on your journey and reward for your efforts."

The hummingbirds twirled and swirled and somersaulted. They formed a circle around the cousins, joined at the wings, rocking back and forth, repeating *"YOU GOTTA BELIEVE, YOU GOTTA BELIEVE."* Their joy was infectious. Harmony had returned to the house in Los Altos Hills.

Hank signaled his charm. "It's time now for us to leave," he chirped with an eye to the clouds. "We are on a schedule. We'll be back in the spring. Goodbye!"

And with that, the charm rose effortlessly into the sky and headed south, frolicking in their lightness of being.

"Who would have thought birds had such gumption," Miles mused, watching them disappear into the blue.

"Don't you just love that song?" Cosmo groomed himself.

"We'll have the best time ever!" Rosie jumped up and down.

"All together," Lexi said with dreamy eyes.

George lumbered around breathing loudly. He was hyped up, feeling impulsive again and getting excited for an adventure. "Maybe New Zealand has pygmy goats, the wild kind," he fantasized. "What do you think, Bailey?"

"I don't know," she said, "but we will find out. What a day we've had. Let's eat!" She bounded inside. The cousins followed.

In the kitchen, Missus had laid out organic, oven-baked, teddy-bear-shaped pumpkin treats for the dogs and salmon patties with cranberry crunch for the cats. Everyone dug in and gobbled it all up.

George mumbled, "What ever happened to good ole hotdogs and bacon strips? They are good for you too!" But he had to admit that he liked the California organic stuff. Life was good. Lexi licked the last crumb from her lips. Her pink tongue matched her rhinestone-studded collar.

It was time to take a nap.

Exhausted from the decision making of the day, Cosmo collapsed on the couch, his paws extended over the entirety of the cushion. Miles curled up close to him, but the idea of the mission kept him awake.

"This could be really amazing," his mind was racing. "Many problems could benefit from a benefit show. Maybe one for the feral cats of Hollywood? How noble! What a future for an artist! But what about those kiwis, those birds without wings? Were they as small as hummingbirds? Maybe a good snack?" Miles bit his tongue. He could not allow himself to think of them as dinner. "No! No! No! The kiwis were endangered. *Parbleu!*" He sighed and redirected his thoughts. Cosmo was on board. That pleased him. They would be together. With warm thoughts of friendship, he eventually fell asleep and dreamt of wingless hummingbirds.

George plodded to his closet for a snooze, Bailey right behind him. "There is a Japanese expression about pigs," he said to her.

"Japanese expression?" Bailey chuckled. "What do you know about Japan, George?"

"They have a saying. I heard it somewhere. It goes, even a pig will climb a tree if you sweet-talk him."

"A pig in a tree? George! Come on!"

"I sure felt like a pig in a tree today. Those birdies sweet-talked me and I liked it," he chortled. "I want to go on adventure with all of you. To New Zealand. Africa can wait."

Bailey beamed with pride. George could be boisterous and opinionated to the point of folly, but today, he was a team player. With a smile on her face, she plumped down in front of his closet and dozed off.

As his cousins settled down, Mr. Guinness paced in the kitchen. He could not even think of sleep. He needed to craft a performance. He needed to innovate, but no ideas came to mind. He drew a blank. To clear his head, he went outside. A walk would loosen his thoughts, refresh his thinking and help him focus.

He strolled all around the property—down the hill, around the shed, past George's crater, along the fence to the cypress grove, beyond the bird of paradise bush, and back up to the patio. The chill of fall was noticeable. He looked up into the November sky, feeling thankful about the gift that had come his way. He could not—would not—disappoint anyone. His new show had to be grand to raise awareness and to save the kiwis. The hummingbirds had given him a start; the rest was up to him.

⊚⊚ Chapter 3: Research ⊚⊚

"BREATHE IT IN, LET IT GO
BREATHE IT IN, LET IT GO
YOU GOTTA BELIEVE
YOU GOTTA BELIEVE."

Lexi popped up from her nap singing. She trilled, warbled and caroled the melody. It stuck in her head. She made the rounds nudging everyone. "You all!" she called. "Wake up! We should practice the new song!"

"Sounds like you know it already," said Rosie. "Repetition is the secret. That's what the hummingbirds said, right?"

Bailey nodded.

"Jolly good tune." George was on board. "Bailey! Help me drill the words!"

Miles and Cosmo, being light sleepers, blinked once. They ignored the frolicking. The morning had been rather eventful. They had more sleeping to do. Let the dogs handle things for the moment.

Mr. Guinness came through the doggie door back from his walk. Energized, he gave himself a good shake from head to tail. "Cousins!" he announced. "We will develop a world-tour-worthy show."

Miles raised his head.

"I thought we had one," George grunted.

"We do, but I want to make it specific to New Zealand, to honor their traditions," Mr. Guinness explained. "I'm thinking five acts: an ensemble song with an audience sing-along, a dance of sorts, a solo by George, an act with local participation, and a thank you farewell music number. We will not rest on past laurels!" He sat down.

"What's a laurel?" Lexi whispered in Rosie's ear.

"It's a metaphor," Rosie whispered back.

"A what?"

"A metaphor is a special way of making a point."

"I can make a point in the sand on the beach with my paw," Lexi murmured back.

"A laurel is a tree. It grows bay leaves."

"Missus puts bay leaves in her soup." Lexi licked her lips, remembering the mouthwatering smell of spicy lentils with onions and garlic.

"In the olden days, bay leaves were used to make wreaths to crown winners. So 'laurels' is a metaphor for success. When he says 'we won't rest on our laurels', Guinny means that we should not be satisfied with past glory. Get it?"

"Oh! I do. He doesn't want us to get lazy."

"You, Lexi. Not me." Rosie winked.

Lexi wrinkled her brow, which she rarely did, and raised her voice. "I'm not lazy, Rosie," she said. "We can't all be like you. You are always active, running around, even when there is nothing to do."

"Lexi! Really?" Rosie began pacing. "You make it sound like I'm hyper."

Lexi giggled. "Sometimes you are."

"Shhh!" Bailey smiled at them patiently. "Let Guinny continue!"

"The thing is we don't know much about New Zealand," Mr. Guinness said. "What would entertain a million sheep? And how do we address the kiwi problem? We need to do some research. Let's see what we can find on the computers."

Since Mr. Guinness's Master was a Silicon Valley maverick, there was more than one computer in the house. Mr. Guinness pressed the power buttons on four of them. The fans inside the towers whirled to life. Before the screens lit up, Lexi's eyes grew large.

"Oh, I know!" she said breathlessly.

"What do you know?" Rosie snickered. "Something you saw on TV?"

Lexi ignored Rosie's barb. "It's in the name! Don't you hear it? New Zealand is the land of z's. They must love to sleep over there! We could sing lullabies for them."

"Lexi! It's not New Zee-land. It's New Z-E-A-land! You've got the wrong etymology. Z-e-a means..." Rosie's eyes became dark and her mouth perplexed. "Z-e-a is ...I don't know."

Lexi interrupted. "Gosh, Rosie! I guess I'm not the only one that doesn't know."

"Well, what I do know is that New Zealand is younger than Old Zealand. I'm sure I read that somewhere. But I've never heard anything about Old Zealand." Rosie's little gray face crumpled and she hid her face in her paw. "Oh my!"

"Ladies," Mr. Guinness pointed to the computers, "just look it up on the internet!"

Lexi, Rosie, and Bailey each settled down in front of a screen and poked the keys with their paws, while Mr. Guinness started his own research.

George watched them and farted. He needed a moment to himself, not in the company of a computer. He shuffled into his closet, laid down and dozed off. In his slumber, he murmured, "New Zealand... sheep... hunt sheep... what's there to do... the unicorns..." While still fast asleep, he sat straight up, howled briefly and promptly plumped back on the carpet.

The cats blinked in irritation, but did not move.

"Here they go with their plastic boxes," Miles whispered to Cosmo. "Don't you hate to have your thinking influenced by something like that? We explore the world with the power of our own minds, don't we?"

Cosmo grinned and whispered back, "We find ideas in observation, contemplation and reflection of the world around us. Then we express them as art, *n'est-ce-pas, mon ami*?"

"If we set our mind to it, we can imagine anything." Miles agreed.

Rosie could hear them. "Come on! Get with the times! Try the internet! It could make you better artists!"

"*Non!*" The cats frowned in unison. "Computers are not the answer, Rosie. Books are!"

"You can read books on the internet," Rosie explained.

"Well, it's still all pre-digested. No one goes to the source any more. Cat culture, may I say, goes back thousands of years. In the Egyptian way of life, cats were considered to be demi-gods." Miles turned up his nose. "Ever since then, we've been thinking for ourselves, and not rehashing pre-chewed and regurgitated information."

Rosie kept on clicking. "It all depends on how you use it."

"Fill us in if you find anything worthwhile. We'll advise and help develop the new show once your research is done." Miles turned his back.

Cosmo, however, forever curious, was enthralled by the screens. "While you are at it, can you do me a favor?" he conceded. "Can you find out what language they speak in New Zealand?"

"Easy." Rosie was eager to help. "I can find out all kinds of stuff."

"Really? Like what?" Cosmo leaned forward, his ears alert, his interest piqued.

"Like… you can take a virtual tour of the universe and see stars up close without leaving the couch."

"Far out! Like whole constellations? Maybe … maybe you could show me that sometime?" And with that Cosmo, also, turned around, curled up next to Miles and the two went back to daydreaming, unperturbed by the clatter of keys.

"Kiwi… kiwi…" Lexi mumbled as she nudged the mouse around with her paw. "This says kiwis are fruit. Kiwi fruits are vitamin bombs. Kiwis … here, it says … Rosie! It's also a sports team!"

Kiwi Fruit on the Vine—
Actinidia deliciosa

Kiwi Fruit

"Shh!" Rosie admonished. "Let me do my own research!"

"But Rosie! Look!" Lexi insisted. "The people of New Zealand are called kiwis too. I'm confused. Help, Rosie!"

Rosie barked back, "Be quiet!"

"How do you expect me to learn stuff when you are so mean?"

"You are interrupting me." Rosie shook her body. "Keep reading!"

"Ladies!" Mr. Guinness intervened. "Can we have some peace?"

"I'm trying to concentrate on Cosmo's question." Rosie was cross. "I was sure they speak New Zealandish in New Zealand, but here it says they speak English. How can that be, when they live so far away? Oh, wait! They also speak Maori."

"What is Maori?" Lexi asked.

"Maori is what the indigenous people speak," Rosie replied. "It says so right here."

"What are indigenous people? Is that different from New Zealanders?"

"Some New Zealanders are indigenous. Some aren't. Indigenous people are descendants of the first known people who lived in any place, like Native Americans are the indigenous people of the United States. The Maori are the indigenous people of New Zealand." Rosie pressed her nose to the screen as she continued her research. "And look at this! There is a rule in New Zealand about the length of names."

"What?" Lexi pushed Rosie aside to get a better look. Rosie pushed right back.

"A name for anything cannot be longer than 100 letters," Rosie read. "Listen to this! There is a hill in New Zealand that has the longest place name in the world. It's so long it looks like a snake: **Tetaumatawhakatangihangakoauaotama teaurehaeaturipukapihimaungahoronukupokaiwhenuaa kitanarahu**. Wow! I'm out of breath."

"How many letters was that?"

Rosie counted. "92!"

"Too funny! Te-tau-ma-ta-W H A T?" Lexi gasped. "Can you remember that? What does it mean, Rosie?"

"It means the place where Tamatea, the man with the big knees, slid down, climbed up and swallowed mountains. He was therefore known as a land eater." Rosie looked up from her screen. "And he played the flute to his loved one." She giggled.

"A land eater who plays music?" Lexi laughed.

"We should tell the cats," Rosie said. "They'll love this."

"Do you think they can say that name in one breath? Miles! Cosmo!" Lexi called out. "Wake up!"

The cats yawned, but when they saw their cousins so animated, their heads, ears and tails snapped to attention.

"Take a look!" Lexi backed away to make room for the felines.

Miles tried to mouth the Maori word. "*Parbleu!*"

"I didn't know a word could be that long." Cosmo grinned.

"What's the longest word in French?" Lexi looked at Miles from beneath her long lashes.

"The longest word in the whole French language?" Miles paused. His yellow eyes rolled up as he thought. "I don't know." He loved trivia, puzzles and riddles. They exercised his mind.

"I'll look it up for you, Miles!" Rosie enthused. "I'll Google it on the computer! You'll see just how handy the internet is!"

Miles shrugged his shoulders as Rosie turned to the keyboard, but he could not hide his interest.

"I found it! Here! You read it!"

"My pleasure." Miles approached the screen.

"Can you say *that*?" Rosie opened her eyes wide.

"Anticonstitutionnellement," Miles purred. "I don't know what it means, but I love the way it sounds." His tail twitched back and forth.

Mr. Guinness had been listening to his cousins while conducting his own search—pulling up multiple screens, scrolling through websites, letting images blink at him, until finally...

"Excellent! I've got it!" He threw up his front paws and turned around. "Bailey, everyone! Please, come! Someone wake up George!"

"What is it?"

"I found a Maori story about the kiwis," Mr. Guinness said.

"The sports team?" Lexi asked.

"The kiwi birds." Mr. Guinness smiled at his cousins. He nudged the computer screen in Bailey's direction. "Please, read it out loud!"

Bailey skimmed the first paragraph and looked at Mr. Guinness, with wide open, skeptical eyes. Then she looked back at the screen. "Shall I?" She raised her shoulders.

"Yes!" he insisted. "Of course!"

"Those names!" Bailey said. "Rosie was not kidding about long names."

"Ninety-two letters and then some?" Rosie giggled.

Bailey smiled. "Almost," she said. "I could shorten them. Make up nicknames."

Mr. Guinness shook his head. "No, leave them intact."

"Keep it real," George joined them.

"I'll do my best," Bailey sat down and began to read—the cats, Lexi, Rosie, Mr. Guinness, and even George were at full attention. "The story is called 'Why the Kiwi Lives on the Forest Floor.'"

"Why does he?" George asked.

"She's getting to that." Rosie hopped up and down.

Bailey cleared her throat. "One day, a long time ago, the Master of the Forest, Tane-mahuta, was walking through the woods. He noticed that his trees looked sick. A plague of insects that lived on the forest floor was eating them. Tane-mahuta told his brother Tane-hokahoka, the Master of the Sky, Storms and Wind, what was happening to the trees. Tane-hokahoka decided to help his brother. He called on all the birds to come for a meeting. Tane-mahuta said to them:

'The ground bugs are eating all the trees. They are destroying them. I need one of you birds to give up your life in the sky and in the tree tops to come and live down on the forest floor and eat these bugs, so the trees will be saved. Who will do this?' Tane-mahuta and Tane-hokahoka waited and listened." Bailey paused and took a deep breath before she continued. "Not a single bird spoke up. Tane-hokahoka turned to Tui. 'Tui, will you come down from the forest roof?'

Tui said, 'Oh no, Tane-hokahoka—it is too dark down there. I'm afraid of the dark.' Tane-hokahoka turned to Pukeko. 'Pukeko, will you forget about blooms and sweet berries and come down from the forest roof to eat the bugs?'

Tui—*Prosthemadera novaeseelandiae*

Pukeko said, 'Oh no, the ground is too damp. I don't like getting my feet wet.'

Tane-hokahoka then turned to Pipi-wharauroa and asked, 'Pipi-wharauroa, will you come down from the forest roof?'

Pukeko—*Porphyrio melanotus*

Pipi-wharauroa said, 'Oh no, I'm too busy building a nest for my family high up in this tree.'

Pipi-wharauroa—*Chrysococcyx lucidus*

Tane-hokahoka knew that if none of the birds came down from the forest roof, all the trees would die, and the birds would have nowhere to live. At last, Tane-hokahoka turned to Kiwi and said, 'Please, will you come down and save the trees?'

Kiwi looked around at his family and at the open sky. He then looked at the cold damp earth and turned to Tane-hokahoka and said, 'Yes.'"

Bailey looked up from the screen and at her cousins. All sat at attention, eyes wide open, mesmerized, soaking up the story. Lexi teared up.

"You are a wonderful reader." Mr. Guinness praised Bailey. "Please, continue!"

Bailey shook out her blonde fur and focused once again on the screen. "Tane-mahuta," she said, "the Master of the Forest, and Tane-hokahoka, the Master of the Sky, Storms and Wind, were very happy, because this little bird would save the trees. Tane-mahuta said, 'Kiwi, if you do this, you will have to grow strong legs and lose your beautiful wings and colorful feathers so you blend in with the color of the forest floor. You will not be able to return to

47

the forest roof and will never see the light of day again.' Kiwi took one last look at the sun and whispered a quiet 'Goodbye.'"

Sobbing softly, Lexi said, "I love the kiwis."

"Gosh!" George grunted and swallowed hard. "How gutsy!"

Kiwi Bird—*Apteryx mantelli*

"There is more." Bailey continued. "Tane-hokahoka turned to the assembled birds and said, 'Tui, because you were too scared, from now on you will wear two white feathers at your throat as the mark of a coward. Pukeko, because you did not want to get your feet wet, you will spend the rest of your life in the swamp. Pipi-wharauroa, because you were too busy building a nest for your own family, you will never build another nest again. Instead, you will have to lay your eggs in other birds' nests. But you, Kiwi, you will become the most well known and most beloved bird of all.'"

"Those brave kiwis!" Lexi wept. Her champagne colored hair shook. "What they did! We absolutely must save them."

George sat down by her. "We will," he said with a deep voice and licked her back to comfort her. "The kiwi is a hero. We must act!"

"Who are these New Zealand Masters of the Forest and Sky?" Rosie wondered. "Do they really have so much power? Guinny! Do you believe this? It's not really true, is it? It's a tale someone made up. It's a myth, right?"

"True or not true, it's so sad," Lexi lamented and buried her nose in George's shoulder. "These birds were so kind and offered their wings to save the trees. "And now, when they are in danger, they cannot fly away! What can we can do?"

"Injustice!" George howled.

Bailey kept her cool. She turned to Mr. Guinness. "Could we use this story for our show?"

He gave her a big toothy grin. "Excellent, Bailey! Just what I was thinking."

Rosie said, "Could Bailey recite the story like she did just now? She's really good with the pronunciation, the emphasis and the pauses."

"Thank you." Bailey was pleased.

"You were great, Bailey," George concurred. "But where's the action?" He walked around with furrowed brow. "A good show must have action. Lots of it."

Miles stared at the ceiling, focusing on what to make of this. Cosmo sat close by.

"May I make a suggestion?" Mr. Guinness was inspired. "What if we took the story and turned it into a play?" He focused on Miles. "Miles, could you help?"

"Indeed, I could," Miles purred. "Pleased to be asked. But may I first speak with you in private?"

"Why?" Rosie asked. "What's going on?"

Lexi retreated under the couch. "Why does it need to be secret?" She did not like secrets.

"Just give us a moment." Mr. Guinness and Miles went to the kitchen. After a few minutes, they returned to the living room, smiling triumphantly.

"We have an action plan." Mr. Guinness cleared his throat. "Bailey's reading performance is excellent."

Bailey wagged her tail.

"We know that," Rosie said. "You did not have to leave us to figure that out."

"Ahh! But wait! There is more!" Miles continued where Mr. Guinness left off. "We will introduce a theatrical feature, an action element." He winked at George and paused for effect. "As a special form of dramatic entertainment, *mes amis*, my fellow *artistes*, we shall perform a pantomime with Bailey in the role of narrator."

"A pantomime? What is that?" Lexi poked her head out from under the couch.

"In a pantomime, actors express meaning with body movements. While Bailey narrates, we, as performers, will act out the drama silently."

"Like TV, but with the sound muted?" Lexi asked.

"Sort of," Miles said. "We will accompany Bailey's words with gestures that show what's going on in the story. And it would be perfect for a noisy audience."

"Oh! Miles!" Rosie hopped up and down on the spot. "Will you teach us to pantomime?"

"Yes," he said. "And we will need to rehearse. We need six actors."

"That's perfect! We are six," Rosie noted. "With Bailey we are seven."

"But ..." Miles paused, "to make it truly spectacular and to heighten the drama, we could have it all underscored by a low volume chant."

George's ears perked. "Chant?"

"Yes, George." Miles smiled.

George grinned his widest grin.

Mr. Guinness rubbed his pale belly with delight. "Time for role assignment!" he announced.

"You mean who plays what part?" Bailey asked.

"Exactly," Mr. Guinness replied.

"That's what you figured out in your secret meeting, didn't you?" Rosie danced on all fours.

"Yes. We have an idea of who should play which part, and hope everyone agrees with our casting. We think Miles..." Mr.

Guinness extended his forepaw in a grand gesture, "should take the role of the Master of the Sky, Storms and Wind."

Miles nodded. "And I propose Guinny for the role of the Master of the Forest."

There was no objection from the cousins. Who would play the three non-obliging birds and who would get the key role: the kiwi bird?

"Cosmo," Miles turned to his buddy, "will you play Tui? You are not afraid of the dark, but you do know about anxiety. You understand Tui's fear and could act it out with empathy."

Cosmo grinned. "*Bien sur, mon ami. Je suis Tui.*"

"Rosie, you hate baths and dislike getting your feet wet for any reason. Will you play the bird, Pukeko?"

Rosie hopped up and down on the spot, her ears flopping in her excitement. "Yeah! Pukeko! That's me."

"George, of course, we would like you to chant." And Miles continued, "will you also take the role of Pipi-wharauroa, the bird with the longest name?"

"Pleasure!" George was flattered.

"Can you handle dual functions in the pantomime—singing and acting? I know that's asking a lot."

"I can do it. I won't let you down." George grinned.

"And last, but certainly not least, the kiwi bird!" Mr. Guinness took over for Miles. "We believe Lexi should play the kiwi."

"Me?" Lexi gasped. She crawled out from under the couch. "Me?" she said again in disbelief. "Thank you! We are like a theater troupe again."

"Not *like* a theatre troupe. We *are* a theatre troupe." Mr. Guinness smiled at her. "Hungry anyone? Rehearsal starts after lunch."

⊚⊚ Chapter 4: Conundrum ⊚⊚

A s soon as the last bit of lunch was gobbled up, the cousins began rehearsal. Time was of the essence and memorizing takes a lot of repetition. In the kitchen, Miles worked with his cousins individually so he could teach them the moves, gestures, and facial expressions their roles demanded. George was first. He needed extra time. Mr. Guinness practiced the narration one-on-one with Bailey. He directed her to speak slowly with plenty of delay to give the actors time to perform the pantomime.

While Lexi and Rosie waited for their turn with Miles, Rosie clicked around on the computer keyboard. Studious and curious, she wanted to find out more about New Zealand's pukekos.

"Guinny!" she blurted out. "Look!" She hopped up and down like a spring. "Come here! You need to see this!"

"Don't interrupt us, please." Mr. Guinness said with a soft voice. "Don't get distracted. Focus on your part, Rosie."

"But Guinny!" she insisted. "Come look!" She moved over to show him the full screen. "It says here that in New Zealand, animals have rights."

"Rights?" Mr. Guinness opened his eyes wide. "Rights are important. Rights guarantee that we live together with respect and dignity." Mr. Guinness was on a roll. "Rights must be protected and safeguarded. Rights are ..."

"Guinny!" Rosie interrupted. "I know what rights are. This is about 'rights of non-humans.'" Rosie choked. "New Zealand has passed Non-Human Rights Laws. And non-humans... Guinny..." Rosie was getting emotional. "Non-humans are animals. Non-humans are us."

"This is extraordinary," Mr. Guinness exclaimed. "This is big. Has this ever been done before—to recognize and protect the rights of animals?!"

"Is that *all* animals?" Lexi was perplexed. "Wouldn't that include the kiwis, too? Does that mean kiwis are safe?"

Mr. Guinness looked at Lexi and then at the screen. "Let's find out more."

The cousins gathered around the computer. Miles emerged from the kitchen with George in tow, wondering about the sudden commotion.

"According to this," Mr. Guinness read straight from the monitor, "animals have five basic rights. Number one, the right to good food and clean water. Number two, the right to a good home. Three, the right to behave naturally, according to the way they are made. Four, the right to be treated with kindness. And five, in case they are sick, animals have the right to be taken to the vet to receive medical care."

"*Merveilleux!*" Miles said.

"Don't you love it?" Lexi's eyes sparkled.

"This is about us, all of us," George agreed.

Mr. Guinness checked over the text. "Amazing," he thought. "Rights for animals? What kind of a country is New Zealand?" He walked back and forth, scratching his head.

"Maybe the hummingbirds are wrong about the situation," Rosie wondered. "They said themselves they've never actually been to New Zealand."

"Or..." Mr. Guinness pondered, "It's the opposite. Maybe things are not good at all and that's why they need such laws." He put his paw around Rosie. "Maybe these laws were established to protect animals from bad humans, like the ones who ditched you because you are so animated, like those who ditched Lexi because of her eczema, and like those who ditched me, because I'm a pit bull."

"Yes," Rosie sighed. "They thought I was too hyper. Hyper, my paw! I'm the way I am, fricking awesome!"

"Yes, Rosie." Mr. Guinness grinned and sat down. "These animal rights laws tell humans how they *should* care for animals."

The cats sat and listened. Lexi looked out the window. Bailey scratched her belly.

"This is intense, you guys!" George rolled his eyes. "I need to take care of some business." He dived through the doggie door out to the backyard.

"I don't understand," Bailey said, watching the door swing in George's wake. "We probably won't know for sure until we are there. Let's focus on our pantomime."

"But will we be wasting our time going? I'm just saying..." Rosie insisted.

"Nothing is ever wasted," Bailey said. "It's all about your point of view."

Rosie pulled down the corners of her mouth. "What if they don't want our benefit show?"

"*C'est absurd,*" Miles said. "Whether or not there is a need for a benefit show, there is always a need for art. A dire need! *We* are *artistes.* We want to perform. And we will."

"We could just be tourists," George had come back inside, smelling of dirt and autumn air. "Do crazy stuff. Have an adventure. No show."

"Being a tourist is boring." Cosmo huffed. "There's no way I'm flying across the ocean and not be performing. *Bêtise!*"

"Humbug!" George grumbled back.

"I trust the hummingbirds—they know what's going on." Bailey was sure.

"Cousins!" Mr. Guinness wanted to regain focus. "While you were napping, I researched the kiwi history. Before there were humans in New Zealand, in the natural order of things, the kiwis were fine. Then the Maori came. They gave the bird its name. The mess really started when the Europeans arrived on their ships and introduced pests to New Zealand. These pests eat the kiwi."

"Pests? Like mosquitos and flies? Flies can eat kiwis? How small are those kiwis?" Lexi wanted answers.

"We have to go and find out," Mr. Guinness said patiently. "As animals, the kiwis may have legal rights, but are they being protected in the wild?" He got up. "We must do the benefit.

Shall we learn our parts and get the performance down solid? Miles, would you mind?"

Miles grinned. He winked at Rosie, who was up next to rehearse. Together, they headed to the kitchen. As the afternoon wound down, Miles had taught them all. Everyone knew their parts inside out and a group rehearsal solidified everyone's role in the play.

Over dinner, Mr. Guinness put the yellow pad with his notes next to his bowl. He did not mind the paper getting a few stains from his munching and slurping. Details were important for the success of their trip. His packing list had three items: food, anxiety remedies, and a printout of the kiwi story. After everyone had their fill, he proposed, "Let's pack up."

Miles retrieved his mouse leather satchel from behind the washing machine. It was bulkier than normal, and clanked as he slipped it over his head. It contained four hollowed out acorns stuffed with a mixture of crushed, dried chamomile and lavender leaves. These herbs would help Cosmo to relax. Miles had made two for the way there and two for the way home. He also had packed a tiny flask with peppermint oil to rub on Cosmo's paws, some mouse jerky for a snack and pulverized rat ears for seasoning.

Cosmo slung his satchel filled with art supplies over his shoulder. He never went anywhere without them. He pulled on his four blue, paw-knit sleeping socks that fit just right. "Do you have some socks for Lexi? She might get cold feet." He winked at Miles.

Miles scurried behind the washing machine. He always had extras, because he liked to knit. Back home in the desert climate of Hollywood, the nights can get chilly. So he supplied his neighborhood cats with socks. Socks provided creature comfort. "Do you think she'll mind if they don't match?" he asked. "I have four in her size—two in pink, one striped turquoise and midnight blue, and one white with black polka dots."

Sleeping Socks

Lexi overheard him and smiled. "I'll travel in style," she giggled and put them on. "Rosie, do you need socks too?" she asked.

"No, thank you," Rosie said, "I'm always hot."

Lexi considered taking her chew toy, but then decided to leave it under the couch. It would still be there when she got back.

"Are you bringing anything, George?" Lexi asked.

"I'm good to go. If I need anything, I'll get it there. Travel light, I say. No bulk!"

During her breaks in rehearsal, Bailey had searched the house for a light-weight pouch she could wear around her neck, like a St. Bernard who carries a small barrel filled with libation to strengthen avalanche victims. Since she was taller than George, it was easier for her to not drag the pouch on the ground. She stuck in five milk bones, one for each dog, and the printout of the kiwi drama, folded neatly. Miles helped to slip off her collar, attach the pouch, and put it back on. She was ready, and so was the troupe.

As if on cue, Condor Chiara and her squadron showed up. Chiara was tall, but her companions were even taller—giants among condors. Their legs were long and strong and their chests were very wide.

"Look outside!" Lexi shouted. "They are here! And there are so many! I can hear them snorting. Is this going to be fun or what?"

The cats joined Lexi at the window.

"*Merveilleux!*" Miles said in awe.

"Condors are called thunderbirds. I read that in a book," Rosie said. "They bring thunder to the sky with their massive flapping."

"Far out!" Cosmo seconded.

The condors assembled themselves in three groups.

Up front were Chiara and four others. From their necks hung cradle-like baskets constructed out of bones and feathers, like padded corsets. They were large enough for their passengers to stretch out. They were small enough not to interfere with flight. They hung high enough not to impact landing—ideal for a smooth journey.

Behind Chiara's group, five pairs of massive condors, a total of ten, had settled down on the deck. In their beaks, they held on to a tightly woven net made of palm fibers.

A third group of five condors stood waiting behind them.

Mr. Guinness ran outside to greet them.

"Good evening!" Condor Chiara cheered. "We are so glad you decided to go. I know this journey will richly reward you."

"We are grateful for the opportunity." Mr. Guinness smiled. "We will do the best we can."

"Bring out your troupe! We are ready to load up."

Mr. Guinness returned to the house to rally his cousins. Everyone was ready to go, except for George who scrounged around the kitchen for some last minute bacon. He came up empty-pawed, but he did not fuss. Bailey, who had been watching him closely, was thankful for that.

"I'll be fine," he barked. "Let's go! They may have even crispier and tastier stuff in New Zealand."

Mr. Guinness stood by the doggie door as everyone filed out. He was the last to leave. "I recommend a potty break before we take off," he shouted. "Now is the time."

The condors' snorts increased in frequency and volume. Due to the excitement of the impending departure, their naked necks turned hot pink-red and their heads glowed orange.

"Come on board!" Condor Chiara welcomed them warmly.

Mr. Guinness had his own basket with Chiara. Right behind him, Lexi and Rosie hopped into one together, and Miles and Cosmo settled into the third one. They took off their satchels and pulled up their sleeping socks. Bailey had her own Condor and so did George. His was the largest of the group, a giant. George howled with gratitude.

Lexi trilled the hummingbird song like a top line over the condors' grunting and throaty chuckles. In a bit of last minute excitement, the net had become momentarily tangled. But all remained calm. The condors' blunt claws unraveled the snarl without ripping the net. Everyone was finally ready for take-off.

The first tier of condors flapped their wings, plowed the air and ascended into the sky. The second tier followed holding the net in their beaks. The third tier departed last, catching up to establish a very fine formation. The twenty condors provided a triple-decker flying arrangement: Chiara's squadron on top carrying the passengers in their plumed baskets; the middle squadron below them, the safety net securely gripped in their beaks; the third squadron underneath as an extra safety measure. Condor Chiara had promised security and she had delivered.

As the condors rose into the sky, Mr. Guinness caught the wind in his black fur and barked. His heart swelled with excitement. He and his cousins were going to help those kiwis. They were off to their rescue!

As they snuggled in their basket, Rosie shared with Lexi what she had learned about the name "Chiara." It was Italian and it related to Francis of Assisi, a saint, who lived a long time ago and who loved animals, plants, the sun and the moon; in short, all of creation. He cared for the poor, he preached to the birds and tamed a wild wolf. Francis of Assisi had a student who shared his deep respect for nature. Her name was Chiara. Lexi took that name as a good omen. She imagined how she and her cousins would save the kiwis. And everyone would live happily ever after.

In Miles' and Cosmo's basket, the conversation was brief. "How are you doing, *mon ami*?" asked Miles. Cosmo gave Miles a thankful look, inserted his ear plugs, curled up and went promptly to sleep—the aromatherapy as prescribed by Dr. Miles had done its magic. Miles leaned back in the feathers, grinned and exhaled. Their performance in New Zealand was going to be a masterpiece. He was sure of it.

Bailey closed her eyes feeling grateful that Mr. Guinness had so brilliantly organized everything.

And George, being carried by the most powerful of condors, stood tall, silhouetted against the rising moon, with his ears flapping in the wind. He howled with joy.

⊚⊘ Chapter 5: Sustenance ⊚⊘

The condors had chosen the perfect time to fly west—the winds at their backs were strong and consistent. The squadron sailed through the night catching thermals over the water. Their powerful wings never tired of soaring. When the sun came up, Condor Chiara spotted land—Hawaii.

The descent was gradual and the landing smooth. The cousins jumped out of their baskets onto a gray sloping field— dry, hard, and porous. It looked like twisted ropes of stone with worn ridges. Fleshy rosetta-shaped succulents lined the edges of the field. A silvery fuzz covered their sword-like leaves. There was no grass for comfort, but urgent bodily functions were performed none-the-less, right away. Ahh! Relief!

Haleakala Silversword—*Argyroxiphium sandwicense*

"Is this New Zealand?" Lexi asked Mr. Guinness.

"Not yet, my dear. This is the first leg of our journey. We are in…"

Loud clucking interrupted him—some high-pitched and fast, others low-pitched and slow. Mr. Guinness turned his attention from Lexi to the unexpected welcoming committee.

"Nay, nay, nay!" A gaggle of thirteen geese announced their presence. Chattering loudly, they waddled up the slope towards them, rolling their massive gray-brown bodies from one foot to the other: black heads, black eyes, black-and-white zebra-striped necks. Their leader, much larger than the rest, darted forward, spreading his wings wide, waving at the visitors.

Hawaiian Goose—
Branta sandvicensis

"Aloha!" The large goose stopped in front of Condor Chiara. "Welcome to the Hawaiian Islands. Welcome to Maui. You have landed on the lava field of Mount Haleakala. We are the *nene.* And we bid you welcome!"

"Hello and thank you," Condor Chiara said to the gander. "We come in peace. We are passing through on our way to New Zealand."

"Nay, nay, nay!" The goose chorus responded.

"We will take off soon, but could you please help us?" Condor Chiara fluffed her feathers.

"What's wrong with their feet?" George mumbled, his nose close to the ground.

"Shhh," Bailey hushed. "Be courteous! We are guests here."

"Something's weird though," George persisted. "Their feet are not normal. No webbing! They look like stars."

"We will probably see a lot of things that are different from home. That is part of our adventure!" Bailey stayed calm, but was fascinated as well.

"Our feet are perfect for our environment." Their leader had sharp ears. He twisted his long striped neck to look at the hound dog. "They have lots of padding, so we can walk on these sharp ridges. You are standing on lava, in the crater of a volcano." He paraded in front of George.

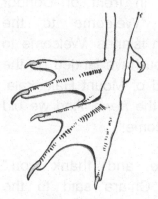

Hawaiian Goose Foot

"Oh... my!" Lexi whispered. "We are in a volcano! Will we blow up?"

"I don't see any fire. There's no steam, or smoke. No flames anywhere," Rosie whispered back. "The ground is cool. The air is fresh. No poisonous gas. No hot stones spewing into the air. Look! There are even buttercups growing in the cracks."

"Cracks?" Lexi winced. "Will we fall in?"

"Look over there!" Rosie pointed. "See the tiny pink cranesbills in bloom? If plants do well here, it must be an okay place."

"How do you know those flower names?" Lexi was amazed. "Have you been here before?"

"I learned them from a book, of course." Rosie smiled. "I tell you, Lexi, reading is awesome."

The leader of the geese stepped forward. "You don't need to worry about eruptions. It's been a long time since the last one. We know when one is coming. We feel it underfoot. There won't be any today. We are safe. Nay, nay, nay!" The gander stretched his chest with confidence. "What can we do for you?" he asked.

The cousins stayed close to Condor Chiara.

"Is it an imposition to ask you for water?" Condor Chiara got down to business.

"Nay, nay, nay," the gander gabbled. "Our pleasure. We have plenty. Please, follow us!" He walked up the slope and his gaggle followed him. So did Mr. Guinness, the cousins, and all the condors.

"How very strange!" said Miles as he walked next to Cosmo. "When they say 'nay, nay, nay,' it seems like they really mean 'yes, yes, yes.'"

"Maybe it's Hawaiian. Is there a Hawaiian language?" Cosmo grinned. "Now we know they speak English here. Does the whole world speak English?"

The procession arrived at a water hole in the lava field. The hole was large enough for everyone to comfortably crowd around. It offered deliciously cold rain water.

"Nay, nay, nay," their leader started up again. "May we get you breakfast? We have leaves, seeds, pineapple, flowers, and sugarcane... the best. But..." he said, looking at the mammals, "this may not be your diet. We also have ..." he paused.

"A piece of bacon? That would be really nice right now," George mumbled.

"May I show you our very finest? Please, follow me." The gander led them to a huge tree with low hanging branches.

"This is our most favorite food—Macadamia nuts. When they fall, they crack open for us. You are welcome to as many as you like."

"Oh no!" Lexi whimpered and hid her face in her paws.

"What is it, Lexi?" Mr. Guinness raised a brow.

"Don't you know?" she winced. "Nuts are an absolute no for us. "No, no, no! Nuts can make us sick. The right food can be like medicine, but the wrong food is like poison."

"How do you know that?" Rosie asked.

"That's what the vet said." Lexi knew that her eczema flared up if she ate the wrong thing and that she stayed healthy by eating the right food for her body. She stepped forward to face the gander. "We must decline your very generous offer, but nuts are not good for us dogs," she said. "I don't know about you two." She looked at Miles and Cosmo, who shrugged. She turned back to the gander. "I do not want to be impolite."

"It's better to be safe than sorry," Mr. Guinness agreed. Mr. Guinness was intrigued by Lexi's demeanor. She surprised him with her assertiveness, but then again, food was her favorite subject.

"I'll eat 'em! I'd like to try," George boasted. "I can eat anything. I ate a toner cartridge once. Maybe I'll go nuts about your nuts."

"You do have an iron stomach, George, but we should be careful on this trip."

George grudgingly agreed with Bailey.

The gander smiled. "Nay, nay, nay! Not a problem. May I offer you something else then?" he asked. "We live in a food paradise. How about some ualas? Another favorite of mine. We dug them up just a few days ago—the tubers have had plenty of time to dry. That makes them sweet. Would you like a taste?"

Uala Plant—*Ipomoea batatas*

Mr. Guinness looked to Lexi for confirmation and then nodded. "Yes. Thank you. We would."

"Come follow me!" With a bounce in his step, the gander started waddling. Again, his gaggle, the cousins and the flock of condors trailed close behind.

Lexi liked walking after the long flight, but the rough lava hurt her paws. She raised a brow. "How far for those ualas? Uala rhymes with koala. I've seen koalas on TV. They are cuddly bears." She giggled.

"You and your TV watching!" Rosie prodded.

Going up the hill, the gander turned around and waddled backwards so he could address his guests as they walked. "Uala is a sweet potato. Very nutritious. It is a Hawaiian staple of the best quality."

"If they are hungry or curious enough," Mr. Guinness thought, "they'll eat uala today." He was not worried about his troupe. He knew Bailey had extra provisions for the dogs and Miles had packed snacks for Cosmo and himself.

The gander and his gaggle stopped at a patch of heart-shaped leaves with pinkish-purple flowers that crept along the ground.

"These look like morning glories to me," said Bailey. "We have them at home, but we don't eat them."

George was panting heavily. "Is this it?" He grunted.

"Nay, nay, nay." With his feet, the gander cleared away the vines and uncovered the tubers hidden beneath: purple, white and orange, small and large, all oblong. He extended a wing and invited his guests to sit. "Please! Help yourself."

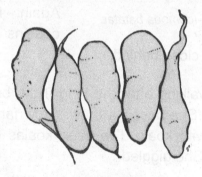

Uala Tubers

"Thank you," Mr. Guinness spoke for his group. He selected one from the pile and took a bite. Not like a carrot, not like a radish, but crunchy and sweet. "Mmm! Not bad."

Bailey took a mouthful. She closed her eyes and started chewing. Then she rubbed her white tummy. "Yummy," she said. "Oh, George, have some. They are delicious."

George grinned. "Why not?" He looked at the uala. "Heck, yeah."

Everyone dug in.

"This is lovely!" Lexi cheered. "Today, we're all vegetarians."

"It's so cool to try a new food," Rosie agreed.

Bailey pointed at the pouch around her neck. "Does anyone want some of this, too?"

Mr. Guinness swallowed his mouthful of food. "I say save it for later."

While the cousins were feasting, the condors had kept to themselves, grunting softly. The gander walked over and offered them ualas as well. Condor Chiara smiled and shook her head.

"Thank you," she said, "But no, thank you. We are scavengers. We only eat dead animals. We like all kinds of rotting meat: beached whales, deer corpses, and dead fish."

"Oh!" Lexi cringed and squeezed her eyes shut.

"We rid the earth of decay. We are like the clean-up crew of the world."

Lexi exhaled gently. "Oh! We love our earth to be fresh and tidy."

Condor Chiara fluffed her wings. "Thank you for the water. It was refreshing."

The gander smiled back. "You are welcome to it anytime. Nay, nay, nay. What takes you south? Are you all migrating? We have never left our island, but we know about travelers. They often stop here to rest and to talk. The arctic terns that breed in Iceland and the Arctic Circle in the summer—they fly south when winter hits up there. And when winter comes to the south, they fly back north. They migrate because they love summer—summer *all the time.*"

"Our passengers are performers on a mission." Condor Chiara extended her right wing toward the cousins. "They want to help a special bird in New Zealand, a bird without wings, called kiwi."

"You don't say," the gander replied. "Sometimes we, too, have chicks that hatch without wings. But we take care of them. They make great nannies. They tend to our babies when we are out foraging, and..." he chuckled, "dancing during a full moon."

"So good you care for your kin. But New Zealand's kiwis have no protection and are on the verge of extinction," Chiara lamented. "Our mission is to save them. We must get going."

"I wish you great success in your noble endeavor, nay, nay, nay," the gander said. "May I ask..." with a nod to the large canines in particular, "will you get there in one swoop?"

"We condors are strong. Our endurance is unparalleled. We will be in New Zealand tomorrow. Thank you for your hospitality."

"Nay, nay, nay," gaggled the geese in chorus.

"This time, I'm sure, they mean 'bon voyage,'" speculated Miles.

Cosmo nodded. "Figure you're right."

Condor Chiara led the group back down the hill to their landing site. She raised her head to check the direction and velocity of the wind. The squadron assembled into their line-up. Chiara gestured for the cousins to hop into their baskets. They nestled in for the second leg of their voyage. The condors lifted themselves into the air once again.

Flying in formation across the Pacific Ocean, the condors used the sun, the stars and the earth's magnetic field to navigate and stay on course. When they crossed the equator, not one of the sleeping troupe noticed that they had entered the southern hemisphere.

@@@ Chapter 6: Arrival @@@

"I see land!" Mr. Guinness called out.

The North and South Islands of New Zealand were in sight. Amidst the vast expanse of the blue ocean, the two land masses lined up in the shape of a giant bird wing. Brilliant strips of beach marked the border between sea and land. Foam splashed against the rocks on the shoreline, some of them bare copper brown and some emerald green with moss. A splendid scene in the early afternoon sun.

Swoosh.

The condors began a gentle descent. The white plumage on the underside of their black wings caught the air for a precise landing. Grunting and snorting, the squadron touched down—a running landing in a perfectly orchestrated formation. They came to a stop in a wide meadow at the bottom of a hill, where their passengers disembarked.

With a swift nod, Condor Chiara dismissed her fellow condors, including the safety crew. They took off in haste. The enormous birds had lost weight on the long flight over and they needed to replenish. This was their time to scavenge for decayed sea lions, seals and rats.

The cousins stretched and rubbed their eyes. They yawned to pop their ears. It was high time for number one and number two. Sniffing around in the grass, the cousins searched for the best spot. Ahhh! The relief! Thank you! And quickly they returned to huddle around Chiara.

"Welcome to New Zealand." She stood up straight. "This is the South Island, near a city called Christ Church, not far from the sea."

"Looks a lot like our farm in Pennsylvania. Strange!" George chortled while looking around.

"Hills, white fences, a shed, barns, a meadow with wild daisies and dandelions. The place seems like home," Bailey agreed.

"Listen!" Lexi's ears perked up. "The birds sound different. What's that drumming up there in the trees? Are those rattling sounds? Are they chimes?"

"Where are the waterfalls, the geysers and the glaciers we read about?" Rosie asked Mr. Guinness.

"What's most important is that we arrived safely." Bailey looked at Condor with gratitude. "Thank you."

Mr. Guinness bowed. "Yes, Chiara Mia, thank you from all of us. I trust you will fly us back when the time comes?"

Chiara nodded. "Of course, Guinny. We will know when you are ready to go."

Mr. Guinness surveyed the landscape. "Will someone come to meet us?" If he and his troupe were on their own, he needed to figure out what to do next; that is what an artistic director would do.

"Yes," answered Chiara. "Wait right here. You will be taken care of. Good luck with your mission. Have faith in yourselves and be patient. You are in the right place." She stretched her wings for takeoff.

"Wait!" Lexi called. "May I give you a farewell kiss?"

Chiara smiled and bent down.

"I hope you find the food you like, all that dead stuff," Lexi whispered in Condor's ear, smacked a kiss on her cheek and stepped back.

"I will." With that Chiara took off into the afternoon sky.

As she disappeared into the clouds, six black border collies came running down the hill. They sped through the open gate and surrounded the newcomers, barking up a ruckus. The cousins corralled themselves and stood frozen, eyes wide as saucers, ears back, hair raised, and tails straight out—on alert. Lexi and Rosie clustered close to Mr. Guinness on one side, Bailey on the other. The cats huddled. George did not howl or bare his teeth. He did not even growl.

The cacophony continued, until a tri-colored sheltie came speeding down the hill to join them. He was brown faced with a pointed nose. A lush, white fur stripe encircled his neck, just like a stole. His body and tail were black, and his legs white. His fluffed-up pelt made him look more massive than his short-haired helpers.

"Boys!" The sheltie barked with the authority of a top herder dog. "Quiet!" The six dogs responded promptly. "To your places!" They ran to the wire fence. "Sit!" They sat with their eyes fixated on Mitch. Out of habit, the cousins sat down too.

"Good job, boys! I'll handle it from here. Good! *Keen ay!*" The sheltie nodded to the newcomers. "You all seem pretty well trained, too."

The cousins laughed, which relaxed them, but only a bit. The sheltie stepped up to Mr. Guinness.

"Welcome, travelers!" he said. "I heard you approaching, while I was up the-ere on the hill. Then I saw you land. Condors with passengers? That's a new one. *Choice, bro!*" He paused to exhale. "The name is Mitch. I run this sheep farm together with my boys here." He gestured to the six herder dogs sitting at attention. "They get loud when they're working, but they'll treat you with respect."

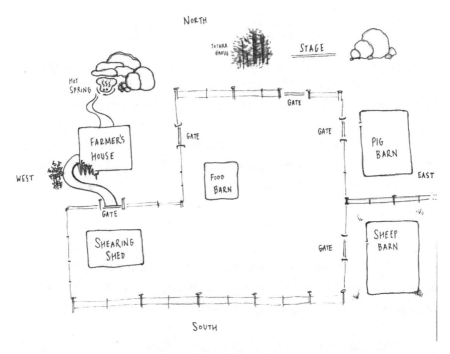

Map of the Sheep Farm

Mr. Guinness felt the tension leave his body. "Thank you." He stepped forward. "My name is Mr. Guinness. This is my family." With a sweep of his paw, he presented his troupe.

"Rosie, Lexi and I are from northern California." Rosie hopped up and down and Lexi curtsied. "Bailey and George are from Pennsylvania." Bailey smiled. George cleared his throat a couple times, sat straight and turned his head, ears down, as if posing for a portrait. He resisted the urge to scratch his belly. Mr. Guinness pointed to the cats and continued his introduction. "Miles and Cosmo are from Hollywood." The cats sat very still, hardly breathing. They were two tom cats in a horde of dogs, after all.

Mitch looked at them, stretched his shoulders and raised his brows. "I wish you welcome, *ay*! A hearty welcome to you, mates! Indee-eed."

"Thank you." Mr. Guinness was all smiles.

"We have lots of sight-seers walk in as spring gets going. But you don't seem like the tourists that pull up over there." Mitch pointed to the farmhouse on the west side of the meadow.

"Spring?" Lexie whispered to Bailey. "It's November. Winter is coming. So why can I smell the daffodils over there? Who is confused here—him or me?"

Bailey covered her mouth with her paw and whispered back. "We are in the southern hemisphere of the earth. It's all opposite. They have summer when we have winter. They have spring when we have fall. By being here, we get to experience spring twice this year. Imagine that!"

"Feels like being in a twilight zone," Cosmo commented.

"Listen to Mitch!" Rosie whispered. "He speaks English, but it sounds funny, like he's talking with his mouth closed."

"It's like familiar music, but played in a different key," Miles agreed. Rosie stared at Miles with immense eyes. She marveled at the comparison. How well he could think! What an intelligent cat!

"You dropped in just to see us?" Mitch grinned.

"We are artists." Mr. Guinness gestured to the sky. "Our friends in high places brought us here on a mission."

"Of course, that's who you are! Now I get it!" Mitch exclaimed. "Yesterday, the albatrosses flew in and announced a special arrival. *That's you!* A mission? We-ell, you have me curious! But first you must be hungry."

Mr. Guinness nodded. His stomach was growling. "We have come a long way."

"May I invite you to food and drink, *ay*? Then we can hea-eer all about it, ya?"

Mr. Guinness smiled. "Thank you. That would be wonderful."

"Ya!" Rosie jumped up and down.

Lexi's ears perked up.

"Starved!" George roared.

"Follow me! Dinner's over there." Mitch nodded toward the shearing shed, a bright red hut on the west side of the meadow.

Mr. Guinness got up to follow Mitch. "What a gracious host!"

"I wonder what their cuisine is like, *mon ami*," said Miles to Cosmo. "I do hope it's not from a plastic sack, *s'il vous-plaît*! But I am hungry. Glad we brought our spice." Cosmo always carried pinches of powdered rat ears to flavor any dull food or unsavory vittles they might encounter.

As the group moved from the landing area toward the shed, an orange tabby cat came strutting out of the barn on the east side. Mitch called out. "Hey, Leo!" He ran to greet the cat. "You won't believe this! This is who the albatrosses were talking about! Come over and meet them! They say they are artists. Fascinating, actually."

"What do they wa-ant?" Leo eyed the visitors with curiosity.

"They're on a mission. Don't *hanker* to guess."

"Mission?" Leo grinned. He bent forward and whispered in Mitch's ear. "Like missionaries? We don't need to be converted. We are fine as we are, *sweet as stink, fella*." Leo checked his claws and licked the pads of his paws.

Mitch turned to the cousins who were waiting, all eyes and all stomachs. "May I introduce Leo, my partner? Leo is in charge of food barn management, night security, and pest control. I could not run this farm without him."

Bailey whispered to Guinness, "Dogs and cats work together in New Zealand just like we do? I like that."

Mitch continued, "Leo, these are our guests: Mr. Guinness, Miles and Cosmo, Lexi, Rosie, Bailey and George."

Leo liked company. Company invigorated him to no end. He waved. "Welcome to our place, ay!"

Mitch and Leo

Miles, with graceful poise, stepped forward and bowed deeply to Leo. Cosmo did, too. In their best French, both said, "Bonjour!" Miles wished he had brought gifts, but in their haste leaving California, he forgot. Feeling regret, he resolved to make a gift for their hosts during their stay, something that might please them, something really awesome.

When Lexi's eyes met Leo's, she gasped. "You seem so familiar. Excuse me, Leo. Do I know you from somewhere?"

"I feel the same way." Leo smiled, then broke out in laughter. She looked like him: all lion. Same mane, same fluffiness, just slightly different coloring, Leo having a lot of ginger tint in his fur and Lexi more champagne.

"Maybe you knew each other in a past life," Cosmo offered as explanation. "You never know about those things."

"Thank you for having us," Lexi said with a curtsy. She giggled and blinked at Leo with her long eyelashes.

"Leo and Mitch, I've got to ask." Rosie stepped forward. "How come your names are so short? We read that New Zealand names are really long. Sometimes they are so long that their length needs to be controlled."

Leo and Mitch grinned. Leo asked, "How do you know that, eh?"

Rosie was about to show off her knowledge about surfing the internet, but she stopped herself, not sure if these hosts were familiar with such technology. Did they have computers in New Zealand? Did they even have electricity? She wanted to be polite. "Well, we did some research before we left."

"Those long names are Maori," Leo explained. "Mitch and I are of the English tradition."

Rosie smiled. "Oh! You are New Zealanders, but not Maori."

"Exactly," said Mitch. "Shall we go eat now? Leo, you take Miles and Cosmo. And the rest of you, please! Right this way."

Iris—*Iris*

The six border collies had remained steadfast by their fence posts, sitting quietly. Mitch now summoned them. "Boys! Time to eat!" He trotted to the shearing shed, passing by a gate that opened to a path leading to a house. Violet bearded irises, exuding their full springtime fragrance, and pink Canterbury bells lined the trail on both sides. Mitch pointed across the fence. "Down there, that's where our farmer lives with his wife. And this here is our pla-ace," Mitch drew out his vowels. "We eat and sleep he-ere."

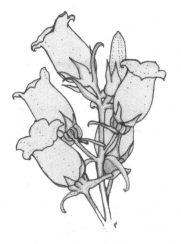

Canterbury Bells—
Campanula medium

As the dogs entered the shed, the tantalizing scent of food hit them. The farmer's wife had laid out a New Zealand feast: meat pie with gravy, yams with butter, corn boiled in the hot spring by the rocks, and saving the best for last—Pavlova, a meringue pie with whipped cream and strawberries. She knew Mitch had more than one sweet tooth, so she always put out extra.

They all dug in.

"This is so tasty," Mr. Guinness commented between bites.

"So generous. Thank you." Bailey enjoyed the food.

"We are happy to share. There is always plenty," Mitch said. "We are thankful for our food, every day." He made eye contact with his boys.

"This is an amazing Thanksgiving dinner." George marveled at the feast.

Mitch looked up from his bowl. "Thanksgiving? What's that?"

"Thanksgiving is a family celebration in America," Lexi said. "We remember the day when, long ago, in America, pilgrims and Indians ate together and got along fine."

"Pilgrims? Indians?" Mitch was fascinated. "Who are they?"

Rosie looked up from her food and realized that she was too hungry to explain. "It's a long story," she said. "But the most important part is giving thanks—hence Thanksgiving. On that day, we celebrate gratitude for our blessings."

Mitch nodded. "Good deal!"

After they were full, the cousins looked around. Seven corduroy beds were lined up against the wall of the room where they had just dined.

"Would you like a tour of our shearing shed?" Mitch asked. Without waiting for an answer, he pointed to a long skirting table made of chicken wire mesh standing in the middle of the room. "The farmer's wife uses this table for cleaning fleeces and separating out the soiled belly wool. What she discards, she uses for mulch in her garden. Nothing is wasted."

Mitch pointed to the table next to it, where a brown-rosy fleece was spread out flat. "Here is where she treats her wool." Beneath the window was an oversized sink with warm and cold water faucets next to a washing machine. "She either washes the wool before spinning; or she leaves it untouched with the lanolin intact. That's her process. We have our shows in the other room," Mitch explained.

"Shows?" Mr. Guinness's interest was piqued. "In this shed?"

"Yeah, in the next room," Mitch said. "We put on shearing demonstrations for the tourists. We've done them for yee-aars. People come from all over to watch."

"Shows? With music?" Mr. Guinness twitched his ears.

"Ah, *mate*, no. Never thought of that. But when the shearing is done, my boys and I entertain the crowd outside with our herding skills, up and down the hill. Lots of fun. We are a curiosity for the tourists, *sweet-as bro*."

Mitch led the way through a red door. The others followed, except George who decided to stay behind and make sure all the dishes were licked clean. Inside the next room, a turquoise platform resembling a stage filled half the space. In front of it was an area for audiences: standing room only.

"The show we put on in he-ere is short," Mitch explained. "Two minutes! That's what it takes to shear one sheep. It's the reco-ord on this farm. Not the world reco-ord though, which is half that, or even less. But our farmer does a nice job—no nicks, no blood, no tears."

Lexi stepped up onto the empty stage and paraded back and forth. "Why do you shear the sheep? Is it like a beauty trim at the groomers?"

Mitch laughed. "Sort of, my dear. But more of a shave than a trim. Just like peach farmers harvest their peaches, we harvest the wool from the sheep. Every spring, the wool comes off. Totally. Down to the rosy pink skin. Good and clean."

Lexi's eyes grew large with compassion. "But then the sheep are naked! Aren't they freezing without their coats?"

"No worries, Lexi. We shear them on warm spring days and then we cover them up. See?" He pointed to the checkered blankets hung on wall hooks. Mitch turned around and headed back to the first room. "Down to business," he continued. He pointed to the seven beds. "This is where I sleep with my boys. Is the straw over there all right for you?"

"Yes." Mr. Guinness and Bailey nodded. "Thank you."

Lexi whispered to Rosie, "No TV?"

Rosie rushed into the other room and came right back. "Doesn't look like it. None in there either," she declared triumphantly. "Maybe they don't have TVs in New Zealand. Think of all the time you will have, now that you can't waste it on watching the darn thing."

"TV relaxes me." Lexi lowered her long-lashed eyelids. "I like it, because..."

"Because?" Rosie demanded.

"I'll tell you why I like TV. I like it because when I sit at home on the sofa, I feel like I'm in the action myself."

"But you are not. You are just a couch potato."

Lexi's lips quivered. "Sometimes, I would like to be in the action. I'd like to do more things. I'd like to be brave."

"So," Rosie interrupted, "how are you going to be brave here, without your pillow, without your chew toy, and without TV? How will you deal with that?"

Lexi tilted her head and glared at Rosie. She shook her mane, shrugged her shoulders and walked toward the door. Speaking over her shoulder, she said calmly, "I'll deal with it just fine. Thank you."

Lexi was gone before anyone could respond.

Rosie lowered her eyelids. "More power to you!" She scrunched her nose, shook her head and plunked down into the straw.

Bailey sighed. Mr. Guinness looked out the window. "In a foreign country, in a strange place, with so many new creatures," he thought, "what was Lexi up to?"

*****

Once outside, Lexi paused for a moment. She had had it with Rosie. Why did Rosie have to put her down? Was it to impress the New Zealanders? Was it to demonstrate how different she was? Or was it just to show off? Well, she wasn't going to take any more of it tonight. Okay. Lexi took a deep breath.

From across the meadow, Leo saw her as she stood there alone.

"Lexi!" he shouted. "Come join us!" With a wide grin, he bowed, turning on the charm. "To what do we owe this immense pleasure? Food over there no good?"

"It's not the food. The food was delicious," Lexi side-stepped the issue. "May I stay with you tonight?"

"Of course. Welcome to my place!"

Leo's barn was a happy place. Enormous stacks of hay flavored the air with sweetness. They were the backdrop for healthy provisions: bags of yellow corn, rolled oats, wheat, barley, soybean and fish meal; large bottles of vitamins and screw top jars filled with fat. The afternoon breeze blew gently through the open windows, making it the place to be.

Leo gestured to a wood plank on the brick floor. "I assumed you would dine with the dogs. But I have more than enough for all of us. My hunt was good today."

Four grey house mice and four brown Norway rats lay there, freshly killed with dried blood on their snouts. A cat feast extravaganza! Miles and Cosmo, culinary connoisseurs, eyed the menu items, licked their lips and grinned. But Lexi gasped and held her breath. She looked up into the rafters, away from the slaughter. "Pheewy. How can anybody eat that?" she thought, but kept it to herself. "Thank you," she said, "but no, thank you."

Miles placed his paws on his hips in a dramatic gesture. "Our dear Lexi is a *vegetarian*."

"She eats like a rabbit," Cosmo added. "Don't take it personally."

Leo grinned. They returned their attention to the banquet.

"*Merci!* This is delicious," Miles said between bites.

"What's that?" Leo asked.

"Delicious."

"Yes, but what did you say just before that?" asked Leo.

"He's asking what '*merci*' means," Cosmo explained.

"Oh! '*Merci*' is 'thank you' in French. Cosmo and I like to practice languages."

Leo was amazed. "You do? I do too! I love languages. I speak Maori."

"Maori? Wow!" Miles loved it.

"I'll teach you Maori if you teach me French."

"Yes, yes, yes!" Cosmo cheered.

"*'Ae'* means 'yes' in Maori."

"*Ae*," Miles and Cosmo repeated in unison. "*Magnifique*! Say something else in Maori!"

"*Kia ora,*" Leo offered. "That means 'hello.'"

"In French, it's *bonjour*," countered Cosmo.

"*Bonjour*," Leo rolled the word in his mouth. He reveled in the new sound. "*Puku* in Maori means 'belly,' and *kai* is 'food,'" he continued. "I hope you have filled your *pukus* with *kai*."

"In French, '*manger*' means to eat. *Nous* mangeons *le dîner à Leo's*. We eat dinner at Leo's place."

The three cats were thrilled. So was Lexi. She was relieved to have some space and time away from Rosie, at least for a little while.

Leo heard Mitch calling from outside. "When you're done in there, come join us out here!"

The dogs had clambered out of the shearing shed. The cats joined them in the sunshine on the grass, as did Lexi. Behind them, a pohutukawa tree was in full bloom with a canopy of brilliant crimson blossoms. There was plenty of daylight left for a conference of the beasts.

Pohutukawa Tree—*Metrosideros excelsa*

"Tell us about your mission," Mitch began, but a loud burp interrupted him. It was George, who grinned and looked wholly unabashed.

"Pardon us," Bailey interjected with embarrassment. "The food was so good. We do appreciate your hospitality very much."

Mr. Guinness addressed Mitch. "We are here to put on a show, a benefit performance."

"What kind of show?" Mitch spoke directly to Mr. Guinness. "Is it like a bird concert? Do you sing?"

Pohutukawa
Tree Flower

"Why, yes!" said Mr. Guinness. "We do sing."

Mitch barked excitedly. "Leo! They sing!"

Leo threw him an amused look and pointed to Miles and Cosmo who had passed out on the grass in a temporary food coma. He took their napping as a compliment on his dinner. His catch had been juicy and plenty.

"Our show," Mr. Guinness continued, "has a variety of acts, including a drama. The drama is at the core of our mission. We wish to raise awareness about the plight of the kiwis and the threat of their extinction."

"It's about our kiwis?" Mitch raised both front paws in astonishment. "The ones over there in the totara grove?" He pointed beyond the farm fence.

Leo stared and his eye twitched. "What do *you* know about them? How do you know about the kiwi killing fields?"

"Kiwi killing fields?" Mr. Guinness raised his voice. That woke up Miles and Cosmo.

"Yeah." Leo nodded to the west. "It's been happening over the-ere for some time."

"We are here to try and make their lives better. At least we hope we can," Mr. Guinness continued. He felt his heart pump faster; it seemed he had struck a chord with these locals. "Hope made us come all this way. Any advice you have is greatly appreciated. Do you think we can make a difference?"

"Wait a minute," Leo turned to Mitch. "Save the kiwis!? A tall order!" He turned to the cousins. "I was a kiwi killer once."

The cousins stared.

"In my youth I was reckless. I devoured kiwi eggs and chicks. Then, in a thunderstorm, I fell from a tree and hurt my leg. Mitch found me and took me in. He nursed me back to health. He gave me responsibilities on the farm, like keeping pests out of the pig food. He mentored me and showed me a new way of life by teaching me that meaningful work brings great rewards."

Miles gazed into the distance. What a confession, he thought. What honesty! What a transformation of life style!

Cosmo stared at the sky, impressed by Leo's candor.

"I changed my habits," Leo continued. "With Mitch's help, I became reformed and left kiwi eggs and chicks alone. It worked for me. Maybe this can work for others too."

Mitch sat, listened and pondered with knitted brow. Maybe he and Leo could do more than just work. Maybe they could be socially active. One does not know what is possible until one tries. Leo's past proved that change was possible on a *one* beast basis. Could this be a model for an entire animal community?

"Could something be done for *all* the kiwis *now*? Something life changing? Is this is naïve? Is this a crazy dream! Can a benefit show change anything?" Leo stood up and walked about, tail erect and wagging.

"Come to think of it," Mitch said to Leo, "why have we not done anything about this problem before? It's happening right under our noses.

"What do we have to lose?" Leo said, matter of fact.

"Right! Right! Right!" Mitch nodded.

"Worst case—things stay as they are. Best case—the kiwis find some peace. At the very least we'll be entertain-ned."

"But come to think of it," Mitch sighed. "When would we do this? We don't have any spare time." He paused. "We work, eat, sleep, and go back to work again. Not showing up is not option. We can't just throw a sickie." Mitch bit his lip. "Enthusiasm for this gra-and idea got us carried away. As much as I would like to do a show to help the kiwis, my commitment to the farm is most important. I have to be responsible. Everyday. No sloughing off. No excuses. No exceptions."

Mr. Guinness understood. As a former corporate dog, he too had worked long hours every day. And when he let art into his life, he experienced even more work but also more joy.

"Having the arts here could improve your performance at the job. The arts are of great benefit. The arts stimulate and rejuvenate the mind. Art works. Think of the possibilities, Mitch!" he pleaded.

"It's not the show that's the problem. It's finding the time."

"Would there be any possibility of hosting the show in the evening, when your sheep are home?"

Mitch's eyes lit up. "You know what? Every week, on Fridays, we bring the herd in early, because there is a party at the farmer's house. He plays Bridge with friends. They get so excited, so loud, so passionate, we can hear them in the shearing shed. Friday night could be it."

Leo smacked his lips. "Keen ay! Let's try it!"

"All right!" Mr. Guinness slapped his knees. He had envisioned cooperation from the locals, and appreciated Mitch's and Leo's team spirit. He wanted to seal the deal and shake paws with Mitch and Leo. "Shall we talk details?" The mission had a good start. "What about a stage?"

"How about the one in the shearing shed?" Mitch suggested. "It's ready to go."

"That would be amazing, but how about somewhere outside? We are hoping to accommodate as big an audience as possible," Mr. Guinness said.

Mitch rolled up his eyes to think for a moment. "What about the hillside beyond the fence? Let's take a look!" He headed to the northern gate, which opened to an elevated area framed by rocks. He unlocked the gate and walked through. Mr. Guinness and Leo followed. The cousins joined them.

"How about this?" Mitch stretched out a paw to show off the landscape.

Mr. Guinness was pleased. "Perfect."

"Never thought this meadow would have a purpose other than grazing," Mitch chuckled.

"I see a grand stage," exclaimed Mr. Guinness. "That large tree frames it on the left. And on the right, the boulders form a natural edge. What a beautiful, organic performance space! Miles, what do you think?"

"A dream come true." Miles was all smiles.

Mr. Guinness walked around it. "This is better than I could have imagined." He pointed to the buildings on the east side. "What are those two barns used for?"

"One barn is for the sheep; the other houses the pigs," Leo chimed in.

"Would they like to come to the show?" Mr. Guinness asked.

"I don't see why not. In the winter and spring our sheep sleep in the barn, but for the show, we can let them out." Mitch was totally on board—New Zealand hospitality in action. "Your audience is built in."

"Could we get some publicity? Reach out to the neighbors?"

"No worries, mate! Our sheep 'bah' a lot. That is how they connect with their relatives. They'll spread the news all over the neighborhood. Who knows, a zillion white sheep may show up in addition to our own." Mitch had it all worked out.

"With such a large crowd, will there be a safety issue?" Mr. Guinness asked. "Do we need ushers?"

"Ay! Ay! My boys were born to usher," Mitch said with pride and Leo nodded. "Ushering is our specialty. So far, we've never had an incident."

"So it's settled then?" Mr. Guinness looked Mitch and Leo in the eye. "We have a deal?"

They shook paws to seal the pact.

Mitch turned around and called his boys. "We must tell the sheep. Go get Angus!"

◎◎ Chapter 7: The Stampede ◎◎

On cue from Mitch, the six border collies took off in a flash, up the hill. The dogs rapidly became smaller and smaller as they approached the grazing sheep, those dots on the grass, barely visible to the naked eye. The team was tasked with bringing the flock down the hill to meet the cousins and to hear the news. With calm urgency, the dogs rallied the herd.

Angus, the head ram, was the first to come into full view. Rusty brown and huge with wool, he led the procession. Right behind him, so close to him her nose touched his tail, was Aliya, a slightly smaller, rose-tinted ewe. The rest of the sheep followed. The herding crew ran around them ensuring that even the last dawdler made it down safely.

Mitch was waiting for Angus at the north gate. Angus bowed down to greet him. The two pressed their foreheads together in traditional Maori fashion. The sheep huddled behind them. Angus raised his head, eying the visitors as Mitch conferred with him. The cousins could only stare; they had never seen sheep like this:

Brown
Grey
Maroon
Silver
Some with white bodies and black heads

Some with white tops and black bellies
Some beige with brown butts
Some white with black butts
Some with black knees
Some with black ears
Some all black with champagne colored butts
Some half black from head to the ribs
And some black from head to tail.

A designer assortment of patterns and colors.

"Don't you love it?" Lexi whispered with wide eyes. "Whoever would have thought such beauty existed?"

With Mitch leading the way, Angus and Aliya walked inside the fence toward Mr. Guinness. The flock followed, watching the newly arrived creatures, their ears twitching and heads turning this way and that.

The head ram greeted Mr. Guinness and the cousins. "Angus is my name," he said bowing his head. "This is Aliya, my partner. Welcome to our farm."

"It is a pleasure to meet you," Mr. Guinness said. He could smell the lanolin on the sheep's wool, a fragrance new to him, almost like honey with a tint of lemon.

"Mitch filled me in about your benefit show," Angus replied. "I love it! We do need to save the kiwis, like the farmer's wife saved all of us sheep. The sheep on this farm support you and will definitely attend your show, with Mitch's permission, of course," Angus continued calmly. "I also have connections to the other farms. We stay in touch with our relatives. We can spread the word and get a lot of sheep to come. I mean, HEAPS OF SHEEP." Angus winked.

Mr. Guinness delighted in Angus's matter-of-fact response. His heart inside his great barreled chest swelled with optimism. The audience seemed to be guaranteed. The bigger the audience, the more impact their message would have.

Angus was not done yet. "We know what's going on. All of us, we are always watching, with our keen eye sight. We see everything, including what's happening to the kiwis. We know about their dilemma and we know who is causing their problem."

"You do?" Mr. Guinness took a step back.

"It's the stoats. Plain and simple. They are killing the kiwis."

Mr. Guinness turned to Mitch with a questioning eye.

Mitch nodded. "No question, mate. It's the-em alright."

Angus went on. "We need to save the kiwis. My flock will start a publicity campaign for your show. All of us can help. We have loud voices that carry far. Thank you for coming and taking up the issue."

Mitch was surprised how well Angus spoke with this foreign dog, a newcomer to the farm, and how quickly Angus had absorbed the concept of a benefit—no long, convoluted questions, no raised eyebrows, no endless debates. Mitch had never seen him so candid and outspoken. It made sense that Angus was open to the idea, considering the brutality facing his kind. A benefit show to raise awareness about cruelty and violence was right up Angus's alley.

Mitch had always wondered what Angus and his sheep were thinking. They were so calm and obedient. Sometimes, he felt that he underestimated them. He had not stopped to wonder about it. Did these sheep really need herding, or did they just like being corralled, ushered and cared for by the best herders ever?

"Guinny!" Lexi whispered. "The stoats are the killers? *They* eat the kiwi babies? Are *they* the pests the internet talked about?"

Mr. Guinness did not answer. He was distracted by watching Angus and Aliya mingle with their herd, fascinated by their coloring and wondering how they would organize a publicity campaign.

"What do stoats look like? How big are they?" Lexi insisted.

Mr. Guinness turned to her. "We will find out soon."

Angus and Aliya were walking and talking amongst their flock, informing them of the coming event, the reason for it, and what it meant for New Zealand. Mouth to mouth, ear to ear, the news spread. Some sheep bleated mournfully, lamenting the kiwis' plight. Some began grazing, chewing, thoughtfully. Some turned their heads to the west, ears up, tails twitching. Some spoke up.

"We know where the stoats live," one sheep said.

"Their camp is close by," said another.

"Over there in the bush," said a third.

"I can smell them when the wind's right," said a fourth.

"They litter our place with bones, egg shells and feathers! A mess!" said a fifth.

"We've have ignored it for too long," said a sixth.

"Don't like what's going on," said a seventh.

"Bahh," said an eighth.

"Not right," said a ninth.

"Need to act," said a tenth,

"Why not now?" asked number eleven.

"We should care more," said a twelfth.

The sheep bahh-ed, and bahh-ed, and bahh-ed. They wailed, sighed and sobbed over the kiwis' plight. Their sorrow grew louder and more urgent.

Before the Stampede

"What are we waiting for?" a teenage ram yelled.

"Help is coming!" another yelled back.

"Save the kiwis!"

"Soon!"

Mr. Guinness stood in their midst, concerned with how the sheep were processing the news. He raised his voice to address the sheep. "I know some of you are upset. And so are we. We came to help the kiwis. *Together* we can do it."

The bah-ing intensified, drowning him out.

Mitch stayed calm, although he had never seen his herd so passionately worked up. He knew the fences were strong.

Angus stayed calm too. "Let them digest it for a minute. This is them processing."

George barked. Bailey sat and watched. Lexi and Rosie huddled together. The cats slipped away to be by the food barn door.

The lamentation continued. Tails twisted. Hooves pawed at the grass. Woolly bodies shook. All heads turned west, where the stoats lived and where the sun was still up.

"We don't have to be sheep!"

"We can do this!"

"Yeah!"

"Bah!"

"For the kiwis!"

"Let's go!"

"Now!"

Young and old trampled. They were riled up. Rallied, ewes and rams bulldozed west toward the stoat camp. Crazed with compassion, blinded by benevolence, they hurled and tumbled and catapulted forward. They charged and rampaged as a mob, like never seen before, landing in one large heap of wool—colored wool that is, all together, arrested only by the fence.

"Good thing that fence is not electric," George bellowed over the noise.

"Actually, it is," Mitch replied. "But the farmer's wife turned it off."

"Off? Why have it then?"

"She's frugal and she knows our sheep are usually mild-mannered, not the breakout-runaways. Not usually." His six workers stared, motionless, but only for a brief moment. With loud barks they encircled their flock, reinstating order.

The cousins were stunned and speechless. None of them had ever seen a stampede like this. Mr. Guinness threw up his front paws. What passion! What interest! What an awesome audience this would be!

Angus, with Aliya at his side, walked over to the sheep pile to inspect it. No broken bones. No sprained ankles. No one was hurt. He flipped his ears back and forth, then lowered his eyelids to hide his amusement under his long eyelashes. "Sheep are powerful," he said simply to Aliya. "There are so many of us in New Zealand. Imagine what we could do if we were better organized! We need some direction. We need a plan."

"This show, this benefit performance is a good place to start," Aliya said. "Let's help these artists. Who knows what will happen? Our lives here are simple and easy—grazing on the hillside, growing wool and having lambs every spring. We need to wake up. This is just not good enough anymore. The kiwi problem is our problem too. We don't like killing. We don't like extinction. We don't like injustice. We need to stand together. We need to stand up for our values and for the kiwis. Good will come from this."

Angus looked at her. She had been his partner for a long time. They had a huge level of comfort, but in the ease of habit, familiarity and affluence they never talked about issues other than the taste of the daily chew, the location of the best clover patches and the weather. He realized that she had strong feelings about life and she knew how to express them.

"We could kick out the stoats," Angus said.

"How?" Aliya asked.

"Force them out with four million hooves."

"How do you know they wouldn't come right back, Angus?" Aliya was a realist. "And what about night time, when we sleep? That's when they are most active."

"At least, we could make them leave our area," Angus said, "make them leave our kiwis alone."

"But what happens further up the island? Kicking them out of here does not stop the problem. That just moves it along. We need a long-term solution!" Aliya blinked with her long eyelashes. "We must invite more creatures to the show."

"You mean other than sheep?"

"Yes! What about the birds that live above the stoats in the totara grove: the tuis and the bellbirds? They could broadcast all over the islands, north and south."

"The owls, too." Angus caught on.

Aliya nodded. "They could take the night shift. We have not even talked about the potential of the sea birds."

Angus rubbed foreheads with Aliya. He cherished her. He admired her practical thinking and her way of considering the long view. She was one smart female and she motivated him.

"Let's untangle them now and brainstorm tomorrow," Angus proposed.

Together with Aliya, he supervised the undoing of the pile. The sheep shook their bodies until all were their normal, calm, cuddly selves.

"When is the show?" one sheep asked.

"Can we still come?"

"We won't misbehave."

"We want to be part of this."

"It will be all good."

"We'll make it so."

"Bedtime everyone! We've had a long day." Angus called out. "We have lots of excitement still ahead of us. Let's get some rest now."

Chapter 8: Local Passion

For the cousins, it had been a day like no other—a transpacific flight to a new country, new acquaintances, new food, new everything. George rubbed his ears and yawned. Rosie yawned too and looked longingly at the shed where the straw waited. They both decided to call it quits and headed inside for the night. Miles and Cosmo were at the point of exhaustion too. They undulated to the food barn with Lexi in tow. It was high time for bed.

Mr. Guinness, however, felt he should keep working as long as the sun was still up. And it was, if only barely.

"Bailey," he called out. "May I speak with you?"

Bailey struggled to keep her eyes open, but she fought off her sleepiness.

"It would be my pleasure," she said. She shook off her lethargy with a thorough wiggle from head to toe.

"Shall we brainstorm a little, you and me?" he asked.

"Of course." Bailey felt her tummy getting warm. She loved being Mr. Guinness's assistant.

"What if we made our new friends part of the show?"

"Aren't they already part of it?" Bailey asked. "They are providing the stage and the audience and..." Her voice trailed off.

Mr. Guinness grinned. "What I mean is having them be *in* the show. As performers."

Bailey's eyes grew large. "That would be wonderful. Let's talk to Mitch. It's definitely worth pursuing. Whether yes or no, it couldn't hurt to ask."

"That's what I'm thinking," Mr. Guinness replied. "They work their routine so hard every day. What if we encouraged their creativity? Maybe they would find inspiration in doing something completely new? Maybe our hosts have hidden passions and secret talents they are willing to share."

"Oh yes! And I think their participation would attract even more locals." Bailey was on board.

"Exactly!" Mr. Guinness wanted approval for his audacious plans, and he got it.

"Imagine the possibilities!" Bailey said. Guinny had such interesting ideas. She admired how thoughtfully he put them into action.

Guinness called out for Mitch. "May we have a word with you? A moment of your time?"

"Of course," Mitch said. "Join me while I lock up the shearing shed. We'll go in from the back side." He smiled. "Your cousins are zonked out in the front room."

Once inside, Mitch invited them up on to the empty turquoise stage. It was a good space to think, to talk and to make plans.

"So Guinness and Bailey, what's on your mind?"

"Please, call me Guinny."

"Guinny it is. So, Guinny, *you all right*?" Mitch asked.

"We want to invite you to join us in our show."

"Well, thank you. Of course, I'm gonna be there, mate. For su-ure. No pro-oblem!"

Mr. Guinness put his paw on Mitch's shoulder. "I mean we want you to perform with us."

"Perform?! You mean like singing?" Mitch burst into laughter. "Not even! I'm not gonna make a fool of myse-elf."

"It doesn't have to be singing," explained Mr. Guinness. There are other options."

"Dancing?"

"Maybe." Mr. Guinness smiled.

"Make me into a clown?" Mitch's body shook with laughter. "*Spit the dummy, bro*! No way!"

"Consider trying something new." Mr. Guinness offered.

"Not in public. Not on stage. Can't be bothered."

"You might be surprised by what you can do. I know I was. I believe there is an artist in you." Mr. Guinness hoped Mitch would be persuaded.

"You are spinning yarn." Mitch looked up to the ceiling, perked his ears and tilted his head to the left.

"Am I?" Mr. Guinness was determined. He so appreciated the reward feelings the arts had given him and he hoped the same for Mitch. "Let me ask you this, Mitch, what do you like to do in your spare time?"

Mitch pursed his lips and stayed quiet.

"What is your passion?"

"Faaa... No one has ever asked me tha-at." Mitch said slowly. He looked out across the stage with a perplexed expression on his face.

Mr. Guinness kept silent.

"You know what I like?" Mitch asked.

Mr. Guinness exchanged a tentative glance with Bailey. She smiled. His heart filled with hope.

Mitch spoke slowly. "I've never told anyone. Ne-ever."

Mr. Guinness held his breath.

Mitch locked eyes with him. "What I love..." he paused, "what I love is fence-post hopping. Do you know how fun that is?"

"No." Mr. Guinness smiled.

"It's an absolute thrill. Once I get started, I can't stop. Like eating crisps. I lo-o-o-ve it." Mitch rolled his eyes. "No one knows about it. I slip out of the shearing shed at night, catapult myself onto the top of the fence post and I hop, from post to post." Mitch began pacing the length of the stage. "I get my rhythm going, solid, steady and fast. It's total exhilaration. The timing's gotta be just right, or else." He fell dramatically to the stage floor.

"You are an acrobat." Bailey beamed.

"Yeah nah bro, seeing the world from the top of the posts frees up my mind," said Mitch. "It gives me a different perspeective, eh."

"That's your talent, Mitch!" Guinness felt triumphant. "That could be your performance in the show."

"Oh shot! How would that work?" Mitch asked.

"I'm not sure, yet. But I have a few ideas. Let's sleep on it. After you bring in the sheep tomorrow, we will figure out the details." Guinny put his arm around Mitch. "I'm really excited about the possibilities."

Leo, curious as always, sensed something unusual was going on. He snooped around until he found them in the shed. "What's up, yeah nah?" he asked and joined them on the stage.

"Leo! Perfect timing!" Mr. Guinness said. "I suppose Lexi and the cats are asleep in your quarters?"

"*Hardout bro*," Leo purred his New Zealand slang. "They are goners. What are you three up to?"

"Actually, we could really use your input. We were discussing the performance and you are exactly who I was hoping to talk to next. Serendipity brings you here."

"You've got that right." Leo grinned. He sat down and curled his tail around his paws. "Lay it on me."

"We'd love for you to be in our show." Mr. Guinness said.

"Whoa—what did I walk into?" Leo, not often taken off guard, was surprised. "Mitch, are you in on this?"

Mitch chuckled. "I'm in, mate. Couldn't resist. Hear him out!"

Leo grinned. "Right, mate."

"Well, let's start with what you like to do in your spare time." Mr. Guinness prompted.

"Hunt."

"Ok," said Bailey. "Is that your passion?"

"Yes! Hunting!" Leo grinned. "Rodents—house and field mice, roof and ship rats, Norway and water rats, and best and biggest of all, the Kiore, known as Pacific rats. I'm a rodent hunter connoisseur and a glutton."

Mitch laughed.

"Anything else?" Mr. Guinness was hopeful.

"Are you asking if I have another passion?" Leo smiled. "Ay! Ay! Ay! Something more artsy? Su-ure! Why not?" He put his left paw on his hip, stepped forward with the right foot, wiggled his claws and grinned. "There is a dance that I like," he proclaimeed. "It's a warrior dance. The Maori call it the *haka*."

"The haka?" Guinny loved the sound of the word.

"Solid Maori. Intense, for sure." Leo winked.

"A Maori dance!" Bailey sat up straight. "That's as local as it gets."

"Would that fit with anything you have in mind? It seems appropriate considering we will wage war on the stoats. You *are* thinking about war, aren't you?" Leo raised his front paws to the sky.

"War?" Mr. Guinness lowered his eyes. "No. War is *not* what I want. We came to your farm on a mission to raise awareness, not to fight. We came in peace."

"How about a small war?" Leo challenged.

"There is no such thing." Mr. Guinness took a step back on the stage.

"Well, alright. No war. I *am* talking about a dance, a dance only," Leo said. "The Maori are peaceful now. They no longer wage war. But in keeping their traditions alive, they perform the haka for ceremonies and for special events." Leo smacked his lips. Maori culture was his thing. Knowing about indigenous traditions made him feel connected to the land he lived on. It gave him grounding in life. "I would love to be part of your show."

"Excellent." Mr. Guinness's brain revved. "Dancing is not my forte, however... Miles and Cosmo tango. Perhaps you could consult with them? What about tomorrow?"

*****

The sun was setting. The sheep were tucked away in the barn. But Angus and Aliya, stimulated by the events of this unusual day, were still wide awake. They lounged outside on the grass together.

"I have an idea." Angus winked at Aliya.

"A fun one?" Aliya encouraged him.

"I want us to be in the show."

"You and me?" Aliya smiled. "How?"

"You'll see. Come with me!"

Angus knocked at the shearing shed door. "Hello!" He nudged the door open with his nose.

Two Hollow Logs

"Yeah, nah bro!" Mitch, Leo, Bailey and Mr. Guinness invited them to sit. "Please, join us!"

"Yes. That is what we would like to do—join you." Angus smiled. "We want to be in your show."

Mr. Guinness was astonished. "You too?" There was more local interest than he had expected.

"If you will have us." Angus scratched the floor with his front hoof. "Also, on behalf of my flock, I want to apologize. They got excited earlier, but everyone is fine now. But it got me thinking. I thought it would be cathartic if we provided rhythmic accents for whatever you are doing." Angus looked at everyone sitting on the shearing shed stage: Mitch and Leo, Bailey, Guinness and Aliya. "What I mean is percussive accompaniment," Angus added.

Mitch was amazed Angus used such big words.

Mr. Guinness put his paws together and clapped with a thankful heart: slowly, deliberately, determined. "We would love that. Truly splendid! Shall we rehearse tomorrow after work?"

Mitch grinned. "Watch out, world!"

Leo cracked up. "Me a dancer! Imagine!" He went outside and strutted across the meadow to his place, jerking his arms in the air and down and to the sides, haka fashion.

Mr. Guinness, Bailey and Mitch joined the other dogs next door in their sleeping quarters. George was snoring in the corner with Rosie curled up next to him. Bailey settled down. So did Mitch. His six helpers had been asleep for a while; sleep was essential for them to do good work. Exhaustion suddenly hit Mr. Guinness. He realized how tired he was. He allowed himself to collapse on the straw, knowing he and his troupe were in a safe place and the outlook for the show was good.

In the food barn, Miles and Cosmo were fast asleep. Cosmo had passed out immediately, so grateful to be on firm ground, and not flying in a featherbed. Miles, very satisfied with their reception in this new land, was snoozing away next to him. But Lexi could not sleep. She licked her paws and thought about Rosie. She wondered why Rosie teased her so much. "Maybe," Lexi thought, "Rosie needs more love." She resolved to love her more, more than ever before, not just with words, but with action.

Leo came in and noticed Lexi was still awake. "Are you comfortable, Lexi? Can I get you a blanket?"

"Yes, please," she said. "I would like that."

He pulled up a blanket that matched Lexi's champagne colored fur. She curled up and he tucked her in next to him.

"Thank you for letting me stay here."

"My pleasure, yeah."

Lexi paused. "Can I ask you a question?"

"Of course."

"What does a kiwi look like?" she asked.

"A kiwi is a short grey bird, sometimes with black spots. It has whiskers like a cat."

"Really?"

"Really," Leo said.

"And they lay eggs like other birds do?"

"Yes. Their eggs are so big that the mamma kiwi cannot eat for three days before she lays her egg. There is no room for food in her belly." Leo explained.

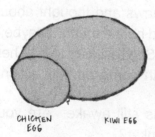

CHICKEN EGG   KIWI EGG

Chicken and Kiwi
Egg Comparison

"That must be exhausting!" Lexi was impressed.

Leo added. "Then the male kiwi sits on the egg until the chick hatches while the kiwi mama recovers."

"Wow! Kiwi teamwork! Do kiwis sing?" Lexi wanted to know.

"They sort of do. It's like a half whistle, half scream. It sounds like 'knee knee'. They sing it over and over. Ten times in a row. That's why the Maori called it 'kiwi.'"

"Could I meet one?" Lexi asked.

"Maybe," Leo said, "but not tonight." He smiled at her in the dark. "It's too late. They live in the deep dark thicket."

"I'm so glad we came." Lexi snuggled in closer. "There is so much more to life than I ever knew," Lexi continued. "I'm starting to feel like I can do more than I have ever done. But then I ignore it, because I doubt myself. And I do that a lot."

"You are so little, so dainty, so charming. I see the lion in you." Leo adored Lexi.

"You mean lioness?" Lexi giggled. She closed her eyes. "I'm so glad I met you, Leo." Just as she was drifting off to sleep, she remembered and whispered. "Hey, Leo, one more thing about the show."

"Yes?"

"Can we invite the pigs?"

◎◎ Chapter 9: Good Vibes ◎◎

"**N**o! Oh no!" Lexi woke up screaming. Wide eyed, she looked around. Where was she? Where was Guinny? She could see Miles and Cosmo snoozing in the corner. But where was George and Bailey? Where was Rosie?

Leo had been awake for a while, grooming himself. "What's wrong?" he asked. "Having a bloody *mare*?"

Lexi stared at him. "Bloody!?" She was confused. "A *mare*? You mean a nightmare?"

"Yeah," Leo said.

Lexi nodded wide-eyed.

"Tell me, Lexi!"

"A monster came and chased the kiwis and swallowed them all." Lexi gasped. "None were left—no kiwi mommies, no kiwi daddies and no kiwi chicks. No kiwis at all. All gone." Tears started falling. "We were too late. Our benefit was too late." She sobbed.

Leo patted Lexi's head. "Calm down little lion," he said, "It was only a dream, my dear. Kiwis live in the thicket over there." He nodded toward the open door. "I see them on my nightly patrols. Last night I heard them stomping for worms."

"Are they far away?" Lexi asked. "I want to see for myself that they are alive."

Leo wondered if he should show her. "Are you up for a little adventure?"

Just then the farmer's wife opened the barn door. She brought milk, butter and dry cat food for breakfast. Miles and Cosmo opened their eyes.

Miles yawned. "Ah! *Très bien! Merci!*"

"Is there any garnish for the kibble?" Cosmo mumbled.

"Sorry. No hunt last night," Leo said. "And no left-overs from yesterday. Not one scrap."

"No problem." Cosmo opened his satchel. "I have just the thing. Happy to share my rat ear powder. Who wants some?"

"Will you join us?" Leo bowed to Lexi.

"May I have a lick of the butter? Then I'll go to the shearing shed and wake up the others. Please, excuse me."

"Tonight, we will have fresh delicacies. How about sushi of Norwegian roof rat?" Leo grinned.

"Hmm … tempting!" Lexi joked. "But no thank you, Leo." She pursed her black lips and stretched her neck high. "See you later." She was curious to check out the other food options. She was also anxious to see Rosie. To be cross with Rosie bothered her. It was not a good feeling. She left the cats bent over their bowls and followed the farmer's wife with her tray of goodies to the shed.

Kowhai Tree—*Sephora microphylla*

It was a cheery morning on the farm. The temperature was spring-time pleasant and the sun was out. A breeze carried the sweet aroma of the yellow kowhai flowers. From the pig barn, Mozart's music wafted across the meadow. "This is a happy place." Lexi thought. "The pigs have it good, too."

By the time she entered the shed, Mitch and his six herders had already left for work. Her cousins were still sleeping. Jetlag had done them in. Seeing Rosie in her slumber, Lexi relived yesterday's argument that drove her to join the cats in the barn. She had never made a point like that to Rosie. Traveling inspired new behaviors. She was proud she had asserted herself. It made her feel good.

"Good morning everybody," Lexi called out. "Wake up! Shall we see what's for breakfast?"

The aroma of warm chicken-and-mushroom pie with onion gravy

Kowhai Tree Flower

filled the air. There was also fresh mincemeat pie doused with tomato sauce, the top crust almost intact; sweet potato mash and slabs of duck pate. The brilliant yellow yolks of the hard boiled eggs, peeled and sliced, rivaled the morning sun. What choices! Lexi was so grateful.

The Meal

As the cousins finished their meal, burping and licking their lips, Mr. Guinness asked Bailey to retrieve Miles and Cosmo. "Have them meet us in the stage room." He turned to the others. "Please, follow me, everyone. It's time for rehearsal."

*****

On the turquoise platform, Mr. Guinness and Miles rehearsed the kiwi drama with the troupe. Bailey was glad she had brought the printout of the story to make sure she presented it properly. When they had finished, Mr. Guinness took George aside.

"I have news," he said. "Mitch has agreed to be in the show and I want to team him up with you. He is planning an acrobatic performance. I think it would be magnificent if you could chant for him while he performs. Would you like to do that?"

George grinned. "Like it? I would love it!" he said. "Though right now, I feel like keeling over, like all my energy is drained out of me. My bones just want to collapse."

"That's jet lag," Mr. Guinness smiled sympathetically. "Our bodies are not used to this time zone. A nap will do you good." George gratefully shuffled to his straw bed next door.

The cats went back to the food barn, but not to nap. They had an agenda: creating props for the show. Leo had given them free rein to use anything from the barn they might need.

Cosmo pulled the art supplies from his mouse leather satchel: short colored pencils, a glue stick and a wide-eyed needle. Its tip was stuck in a peanut and wrapped in rat leather so it would not poke anyone. He slit the seams of the paper food sacks that the farmer, a frugal man, had saved, and cut them into rectangles before fortifying them with a frame of sticks on the back. On the front, he glued tiny twigs in a fancy crisscross pattern. These contraptions would be the signs for each act. Simple, perfect, beautiful.

Meanwhile, Miles worked on a backdrop for the pantomime. With his finely manicured claws, he ripped a blanket to size and fashioned it into a banner. He embellished the top and bottom with red tassels from the wool supply. Fat yellow wool knots lined the sides. He borrowed Cosmo's needle to embroider large red letters using a double cross-stitch technique.

With the banner in their mouths, in parallel step, the cats climbed the 100-foot-tall totara tree located stage left. They fastened the banner to the trunk with strings about halfway up. The trunk of the totara was perfect for securing the banner, because the brown bark had thick scaly slabs. The banner held on just fine. The tassels swayed in the breeze. The cats descended and stood back a few yards to admire their work. It was a spectacular sight of color and meaning. The banner's size reflected the noteworthiness of what was going to happen on the stage. It read vertically, top to bottom:

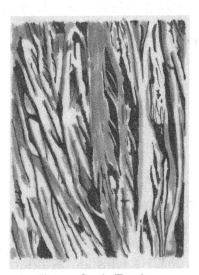

L
E
T

K
I
W
I
S

L
I
V
E

Totara Scaly Trunk—
Podocarpus totara

Totara Scaly Trunk—
Podocarpus totara

The cats hi-fived each other for a job well done and retired to the food barn for an afternoon nap. When Leo came back from his daytime hunt and spread out his catch, the aroma of fresh meat woke them up.

"I have news, guys," Leo said. "Three things. Number one, the stoats are out and about."

"Out and about? Is that unusual?" Cosmo and Miles asked.

"They're more active than normal. They are sticking up their heads from their tunnels and mazes, and hanging around as though they're spying on us. Like they know something's up."

"Should we be concerned?"

"It's suspicious," said Leo. "We need to be on the lookout."

"*Voilà*," Miles pursed his lips. "Our show will be so *a propos*."

"Number two, I saw the banner," Leo said. "Fine work, guys."

"Thank you. I think it's far out." Miles smiled modestly. "We did the best with what we had."

"What's number three?" Cosmo asked.

Leo grinned. "Guinny suggested I join you for a dance. Would you be up for that?"

Miles jumped up and strolled around, tail up. *"Merveilleux!"*

Cosmo scratched his chin. "Our routine is the Argentinian tango. Come outside. We'll show you." He whistled a tango tune and grabbed Miles's paw to demonstrate tango steps for Leo in the grass. After dancing expertly, the cats bowed with a flourish. Out of breath, Miles explained. "Normally this dance is for couples. And we are three. How can we adapt it?"

Miles and Cosmo Doing the Tango

Cosmo gave him a blank look. "Any ideas, Leo?"

"Impressive! You have inspired me." Leo's eyes glowed. "I have an idea about a dance all of us can do. Are you up for something new?"

"Yes, *mate!*" Miles and Cosmo nodded, eager to learn.

"The *haka!*"

"What?" asked Miles.

"The *haka*, a dance like you've never seen before—foot stomping, body slapping, shouting, chanting and..."

"You call that a dance?" Miles was intrigued.

"There is more! You bulge out your eyes and stick out your tongue."

"That will scare any stoat, all right." Cosmo giggled.

"This is how it goes." Leo stood up on his hind legs to snap into starting position. Paws on his hips he bent his knees, slapped them three times, raised one knee upwards, dropped to one knee, beat his arms three times, stood up, shook his body, crouched one leg out to the left, the other to the right, and hollered "*haka!*" He stretched his front arms left and right, bent his elbows, flexed his chest muscles, stuck out his tongue for a grand finale and shouted, "*Haka!*" Again.

Miles and Cosmo looked at each other amazed: New Zealand culture!

"Want to try it?" Leo grinned.

"Bien sûr." The cats were on board. "Will it get loud?"

Leo nodded. "It must! Let's go inside." He closed the doors and windows of the food barn so rehearsal could proceed in private.

*****

When Mitch came home that evening, he met Mr. Guinness and George in the shearing shed.

"Good to see you, Mitch!" George barked. "Guinny told me about your talent. And it would be my pleasure to accompany you." George scratched up some imaginary dirt with his hind legs. "May I see a sample of your performance?"

Mitch grinned. "Plea-asure, *mate*! Let me show you."

He shoved a tall stool into position. He sat down in front of it as if to collect his energy. He then catapulted himself to the top of the stool with an ease and agility that left George speechless. He, George, was, um, too hefty, too big boned and too muscular to do anything like that. "On moon lit nights, when my sheep are asleep," Mitch said, "I practice. I've done it for yee-ahrs." He swished the vowels in his mouth with extra gusto. "I can do even more." Mitch said. "A high plank act."

"Ay, mate!" George tried out his New Zealand slang. He was on fire. "While you do that, I have a surprise for you."

Just as George was about to explain, the door of the shearing shed flew open. Angus stuck his head in. "Guinny," he cheered. "Want to see our skill?"

"Come on in!" Mr. Guinness was pleased.

Angus rolled in two hollow logs, one longer than the other. Aliya was right behind him. Both sheep sat down holding the logs with their hind legs. With their front hoofs they drummed a low, slow, pulsating duet the likes of which had never been heard before on this farm.

"*Sweet-as bro!*" Mitch shouted. "Didn't know you both had it in you!"

Mr. Guinness beamed. This farm brimmed with creativity. He was confident that the show, enriched with local talent, was going to be a smashing success.

☺/☺ Chapter 10: Crash ☺/☺

Friday, the day of the show, arrived. The weather was perfect. The air was alive with all the birds and their voicings. All morning long, the sheep bleated about the upcoming performance. There was no better publicity than this – a sound wave flowing from one farm to the next. Turnout was expected to be grand.

As the evening approached, Mitch and his crew escorted their own sheep to the front—a rainbow of colors. Leo picked the lock of the pig barn and opened its door. The pigs, rosy sows and hairy hogs, bustled out and were escorted in right behind the colored sheep. Soft oinking and grunting filled the air. Tails twirled. What extraordinary fun!

Pigs

Numerous groups of white sheep from the neighboring farms filed into the seats behind the pigs. Mitch and his crew welcomed their sheep neighbors, adults and teenagers alike. They ushered them in early to make it easier for late comers. There were no lambs around yet, since lambing season did not start until July. There was enough room for heaps and heaps of sheep.

The sheep were patient. They could stand quietly for a long time. While still young, they were taught to obey their elders. In case of danger, they knew to stay together, orderly. That was their best defense against air attacks from eagles or kea parrots which were endemic in New Zealand. But on this farm, the sheep felt safe. Waiting for the start of the show was no problem for so many sheep. The audience was ready.

Cosmo's signs for each act were lined up beneath the totara tree next to the stage. The bellbirds, tuis and wood pigeons could see them from their perches and read them aloud to one another.

On a signal from Mr. Guinness, Angus and Aliya began to pound rhythmically on their logs, announcing the start of the show. A hush fell over the crowd. Mr. Guinness ascended to the stage and stood in the center. He took a deep, steadying breath. On his cue, the drums stopped.

"Hello everyone! We are so happy to be with you in New Zealand. We are grateful that you have welcomed us so warmly. Thank you for your hospitality!"

There were cheers. "Any time, mate."

"May I present my family and fellow artists?"

The crowd roared. *"She'll be right!"*

"Please, cousins, join me on stage!" With a wide gesture, he invited up his troupe who had been waiting close by, wiggling their bodies, eager to start. Mr. Guinness positioned himself in the middle, Rosie and Lexi flanked him, then the cats on each side, and George and Bailey on either end. "We are here to entertain you. Are you ready?"

The crowd applauded enthusiastically. "Yeah, yeah!"

"Bailey, shall we begin?"

Bailey stepped off the stage to fetch the first sign. She returned, carrying it slowly in front of the audience, for everyone to see.

Act I
Sing-Along ....**Ensemble**

She placed it by the side of the stage and joined her cousins. The seven stood, evenly spaced, smiling and waving.

"Ladies and gentlemen, ewes and rams, hogs and sows, birds, beasts and fowl!" Mr. Guinness announced. "Back home, our friends, the hummingbirds, taught us this song. It is about our beautiful world. Sing along if you like!"

The audience held their breath in anticipation. Mr. Guinness lifted his paw, like a conductor raises a baton before his orchestra. The cousins entwined their front legs, took a deep breath and began:

YOU GOTTA BELIEVE
YOU GOTTA BELIEVE
BREATHE IT IN
LET IT GO
BREATHE IT IN
LET IT GO
YOU GOTTA BELIEVE
YOU GOTTA BELIEVE.

As they sang *"YOU GOTTA BELIEVE,"* they swayed to the right and to the left. When it came to *"LET IT GO,"* they unlinked their paws, turned around once on their toes, and intertwined their arms again.

The sheep and pigs marveled at how well these visitors could sing. Imagine! Dogs and cats singing together! Even though the sheep in the very back could not make out all of the words, they got the vibe. Eyes glowed. Tails whirled. The birds—of course—sang along, too. Wild applause erupted at the end of the song.

After bowing grandly to the audience, Mr. Guinness winked at George to get the next sign. While Angus and Aliya drummed, George schlepped it across the stage. No haste. No hurry. They had all night.

Act II
Haka: Pas de Trois .... Leo with Miles and Cosmo

To show the troupe's worldliness, Cosmo had written 'pas de trois' on the sign, French for 'a dance for three performers.' He listed Leo first to honor him.

As the three cats lined up to go on stage, a whistling tore through the air. Some sheep turned their heads. The pigs oinked a bit louder. Was that the sound of cicadas, so early in the year? Not likely, but possible. Then the noise stopped.

Chorus Cicada—*Amphipsalta zelandica*

When the cats jumped onto the platform, a hush fell over the crowd. Most of them knew Leo and were thrilled to see him up there. The other two cats presented a curious new flair.

Angus and Aliya hammered out a stormy Maori beat.

The cats began their *haka*. They threw themselves into the steps with vim. They stomped. They pounded their chests. They struck warrior poses. Just as their performance was reaching a climax, shrieks rang out from the meadow. Leo wrinkled a brow. Miles and Cosmo assumed it was New Zealand enthusiasm. The sheep and pigs kept swaying to the *haka* chant and clapped in rhythm.

More shrieks overpowered the drumming.

"What is that?" Mr. Guinness turned to Bailey. "Is this part of the *haka*?"

"Not sure," she said, her brow furrowed. She nervously licked her leathery black nose.

The shrieks persisted. Unease rippled through the audience. Heads twisted to the right and left. Nothing unusual could be seen except, of course, the fantastic performance on stage where the three cats finished their dance to thunderous applause.

Lexi carried the next sign.

Act III
Acrobatics .... Mitch with George and Bailey

Mr. Guinness took center stage and cleared his throat. "May I have your attention please?" he shouted. "May I ask all of you to turn around? The next act will be performed behind you."

The sheep, used to following instructions, turned obediently. The back row became the front, and the front row was now the back. The smaller sheep bahh-ed and pushed themselves underneath their elders to get to a better view. The pigs squealed with delight to be able to move around a bit and quickly followed suit.

Fence Posts

The fence separating the farm from the hillside was now the stage. Mitch and George positioned themselves next to it. As everyone settled into their new vantage points, George began a low-key, undulating chant. As quietly as is possible for a beagle, George sang—no words, just a deep rich baying. He kept it mellow to give himself room for a crescendo later.

Mitch threw George an approving look. This musical introduction added finesse to his act. He sat down next to George, swaying to the song. Suddenly, in one jolt, he lept onto the top of the fence post. The crowd gasped. Mitch hopped down, then bounded up atop the next post. One after the other, ten posts in all. The audience hushed every time he prepared to leap. They cheered every time he landed on top, gloriously.

"Ohhs!" and "Ahhs!" came from the crowd. And, "Go, Mitch, go!"

The sheep loved it that their boss had such talent. The pigs oinked with joy. They could not even fathom jumping that high with such grace.

At the end of Mitch's first stunt, George yodeled in two octaves to indicate the beginning of stunt number two. Mitch hopped up onto the slender wooden plank that connected the posts on top of the fence. Sure-footed, he strutted the whole length, as if on a tight rope. He proceeded steadily the entire way, with consistent balance, controlling his body perfectly.

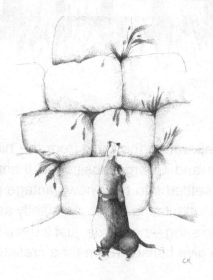

George Chanting

And that was not all. George tossed Mitch a three foot stick. Mitch caught it with his front paws, and steadied himself upright on his hind legs. George raised the decibels. The crowd's eyes were glued on Mitch, mesmerized. Mitch smoothly turned around and, balancing himself with the stick, walked back to the starting point. As a precaution, George walked along side as he chanted. For safety, Bailey walked along the other side of the fence. Her eye for detail and George's bulk were a good combination—just in case Mitch needed a cushion to brace a fall.

But something else was happening. That whistling picked up again, sporadic at first, but then consistently persisting from everywhere—in front, behind, from all sides. Mitch wobbled. The audience gasped. He stabilized himself with his stick and gracefully finished his act.

What were those shadows that moving around underfoot? What was it that scurried about, brushing past sheep legs and underneath pig bellies, quick enough to escape all hoofs?

Mr. Guinness's brow wrinkled. He sought eye contact with Mitch. But Mitch was busy bowing to the applause. Bailey returned to Guinny's side.

"What's going on?" she asked.

"I'm not sure. Everything was going so well." Mr. Guinness's voice strained. "I don't want to lose the flow of the show. Should I ignore it and push on, or address it and possibly make a scene?"

"Not continuing is not an option." Bailey was sure. She tried to catch George's attention, but he too—just like Mitch—loved the adoration and was soaking it in. "We should figure out what's happening and keep an eye on it."

Guinness searched the crowd for the six herder dogs, but they were off scouting the perimeter. He felt his stomach tighten. His paws tensed. He feared losing control, but he could not show it. He needed to keep calm and carry on, as the saying goes.

So he nodded to Bailey and took to the stage. With a regal voice, he addressed the crowd. "My friends, may we have your attention! Please turn around once again. Our show will continue here."

The sheep and pigs had no problem with this arrangement. Moving back and forth, turning round and round made them feel like they were dancing a bit too. As they settled themselves, Rosie carried the sign for the next act.

Act IV
Why the Kiwi Lives on the Forest Floor:
A Pantomime......................... The Septet

As Mr. Guinness reintroduced the cousins as the New Zealand characters they would be portraying, the whistling and squeaking started back up. The older sheep tried to squelch the nuisance with "Hush, hush!" Yet the hollering got louder. The birds fluttered in the trees, restless.

"Can we keep it down, please?!" Mr. Guinness's voice thundered across the venue.

Suddenly, the moving shadows solidified. Small, brown, four-footed, short-tailed critters with white bellies, elongated necks, round ears and long brown and white whiskers appeared. Stoats! Stoats everywhere! They popped up from their holes and tunnels and poured down from the trees. They shrilled. They yacked. They heckled. They yelled. "Coyote! Cougar! Bobcat!" An army of stoats raided the totara tree and attacked the banner. They gnawed through the wool ties and, within seconds, the banner crashed to the ground. They stormed the stage.

Wide-eyed, Miles and Cosmo hissed. Their backs arched with their fur on end.

Bailey dropped her script.

George howled as frenzied stoats squirmed underfoot.

"Do they bite?" Lexi screamed.

"Don't know!" Rosie shouted over the chaos.

Amidst the sea of swarming critters, Mr. Guinness initially froze. As the stoats hurdled over his paws and nipped at his tail, his shock dissipated. The safety of his troupe was at stake.

"Get off stage! Now!" His voice blasted over the noise and cut through the confusion. "Follow me! I'll clear the path!" With his tail between his legs, he jumped off the stage. "Meet me in the shed!"

Barking loudly, he dashed down the hill. He maneuvered through the melee of sheep and pigs and stormed into the shed.

An eerie quiet descended on the farm. A full moon appeared from behind the clouds illuminating the damage the stoats had left behind. The drums had rolled away; the signs were ripped and scattered; and the banner, that poor beautiful banner, lay crumpled in a sorry heap at the base of the totara tree.

@@ Chapter 11: Discord @@

The stage was empty.

The sheep muddled around, mingling and bumping into each other in the moonlight. Since there had been no playbill, they thought the three acts *were* the whole show. They were not at all disappointed, a bit confused, perhaps, but Mitch was in control. He herded his colored sheep back to their barn. Two by two, they walked through the gate. He made sure no one wandered off. His sheep bahh-ed "thank you, thank you, thank you" to him. Never did they see such a fine performance. Who in the world could have imagined the secret talent of their own caretaker?

The pigs were not far from their beds either. They trotted home snorting and grunting, twirling their tails extra quick, boasting in jest that they could do a show too—only grander, rosier and with more aroma. They giggled about having a chorus of dancers with polished cloven hooves and kowhai flower garlands around their necks. They oinked about organizing auditions to find the most vivacious two-steppers. *Their* show would be ready to go in no time. After all, pigs had plenty of pizzazz.

And the white sheep from the neighboring farms? They had gotten their fill, too. That noisy mayhem at the end just added interest. They waited around just a bit, standing, chatting, visiting. Since nothing more happened, they headed home, filing out calmly, two by two.

Mitch's work was done. He waved to Leo who was sitting under the full moon, watching the exodus.

"What an evening!" Leo's tail flicked back and forth.

"Those stoats!" Mitch pawed the ground. "Bloody jerks!"

"Stinkers! Turds! Creeps!" Leo jeered.

"Hooligans! Klutzes! Boobs!" Mitch frowned and shook his head.

"Overrunning the stage!" Leo spat in the grass. "They shouldn't get away with that. They don't rule New Zealand!"

"My boys had their eyes on the sheep." Mitch said apologetically. "They are not trained in vermin blockade. That's usually your department, Leo. But I guess you were rather busy doing the haka." He grinned. "A powerful performance at that!"

Leo groomed his paws. "Yeah! Glory day!"

Mitch chuckled. "Didn't know you had such grit."

"Didn't know you had such gumption," Leo returned the compliment.

"*Hardout, mate,* what are we going to do now?" Mitch cleared his throat. "They never got their 'save-the-kiwi' thing going. Will they want to try again? We may get in trouble with the farmer."

Leo sat and listened.

"We lucked out this time: no broken bones, no lost sheep, no hurt pigs. But *mate...*" Mitch frowned, "I say, it's time for the troupe to move on. Hospitality is one thing, inviting trouble is another. Let's not be stupid."

Leo raised his paw and chuckled. "Don't give up so easily, Mitch! A little commotion keeps mind and body fresh, *ay.* Where's *your* grit?"

"*Mate!* What a mess it could have been! We should call it quits." Mitch moaned. "Too bad for the kiwis, but we have to think about our own flock!" He collected himself. "I'll take another look around the farm to make sure everything is calm, and then we should talk to Mr. Guinness. They're in the shed."

"I'll go patrol," Leo got up to join him.

*****

"Turn on the lights!" Mr. Guinness shouted as he raced into the shearing shed.

"Can't reach!" George barked back.

"I'll do it." Mr. Guinness stood on his hind legs to flick the switch.

"We've been blitzkrieged. Damn those stoats!" George was on fire. He barked until he was out of breath, then collapsed and farted.

Rosie ran in circles with her tongue hanging out.

Bailey crouched in the corner and threw up.

"Let's calm down, everyone," Mr. Guinness urged, panting. His heart was hammering, but he knew he needed to be calm to lead his troupe.

Bailey straightened up, slurped some water from the bowl, and cleared her throat. "I've never been so scared," she said. "That was beyond our control."

"Where are Miles and Cosmo?" Mr. Guinness asked no one in particular. "Up in the tree again? We must find them." He sent Bailey outside to check. "We need to stick together!"

Bailey called up from the base of the totara. "Miles! Cosmo! I know you are up there. Please, come down!" she pleaded. She was still fighting the bad taste in her mouth. "We need you."

There was no answer. The wind swished through the branches. No bird sound was heard.

"I know you are upset. We all are. Please join us!" Bailey waited a few moments before she turned and walked back to the shed. She thought, "They will come to their senses. They may just need a private moment."

High up in the totara, where just yesterday they had attached the banner's top edge, Miles and Cosmo hid out together. Their ears were flattened against their heads; their tails swished back and forth as they stared down at the sorry remnants of their creation.

"I'm done with New Zealand," Cosmo hissed.

Miles kept quiet. Then he said, *"D'accord."*

Their cat pride was as deflated as their banner was crushed. They felt insulted —by stoats. Who were *they* to ruin their work?

Miles and Cosmo looked at each other.

"*Mon cher ami*, we must face reality. This was a total bust," Miles said. "And now our family needs our council. They shall have it. We must make our position clear—we are done. It's over."

Cosmo nodded. They started their descent.

*****

Rosie waited at the door. "Miles and Cosmo! Your beautiful banner! Ruined!" She had tears in her eyes.

"We get it," Miles said, his voice rather curt. "Where is Guinny?"

"In the other room."

The cats went in. Rosie followed right behind.

"*Monsieur* Guinny!" Miles called out.

"Glad you joined us." Mr. Guinness dropped his shoulders. He visibly relaxed. "We need your input, your advice."

"*Quel domage!*" Miles shook his head. "What a disgrace!" Both cats sat down in front of Mr. Guinness, disgust etched on their faces. They shook their heads in disappointment.

Mr. Guinness stayed silent.

"Let's get our stuff and call Condor," Miles stated. "We need to get out of here."

Mr. Guinness was not expecting that. "You want to give up?" He swallowed hard.

140

"We love to perform. But this? We can't do this. Not our cup of milk!" Miles put his arm around Cosmo who shook his head. "We are artists. We accept inspiration from the universe, translate it into art and share that with an audience. We do not want to fight."

"So you see the performance as a failure?"

"Mais oui!"

Mr. Guinness paused for a moment. "I think the stoat attack is a sign of success."

"Pardon me?" Miles asked

"How's that?" Cosmo was perplexed as well.

"Why do you think they attacked?" Mr. Guinness responded slowly. "Why did our performance threaten them so much that they went on the offensive?"

Stunned silence.

"Because, clearly, what we are doing matters to them. We are making a difference." Mr. Guinness's resolve increased. "We will not give up," he proclaimed, then cleared his throat. "I will not accept failure." His voice was firm.

Bailey admired his grit.

"Fine speech," George grunted approvingly. "But how? How can we make something good out of this?"

"First, we need to stay calm," Mr. Guinness said and looked at George with a stern eye. "Then, we need to start thinking."

"Yes!" Rosie chimed in. "Brainstorm and share ideas! Even if they seem absurd. How can we protect the kiwis? How do we free the island of stoats?"

The door opened. Mitch and Leo entered the shed. "Did I hear this right? Get rid of the stoats?" Mitch was almost caught off guard. "This island will never be free of stoats."

"I'm for war!" George shouted. "All-out war! Chase the stoats into the ocean!" He looked around for approval.

"That won't help." Leo pursed his lips. "They are good swimmers. They'll be back dancing on the beach in the moonlight in no time."

Bailey said gently, "May I remind you, George, my friend, if you think about it, the stoats have a right to live here, too. We should not be extreme. Maybe the stoats are not evil. Maybe they just don't know the consequences of their appetite. Maybe they could learn a different way. We must think of another solution!"

"What?" George shook his head. "Bailey!? We've been attacked! How can you be so goody-four-paws?"

"Malice toward none, good will for all. Whatever we do," Bailey said, "we need to think backwards from the future."

"Now what's that supposed to mean?" George huffed. "Have you gone nuts, Bailey? Think backwards from the future? What? The future is not even here yet!"

"Listen George!" Bailey closed her eyes. "Our future is created by what we do today. We make our future by how we act now."

"How do you mean?" George asked.

"Tell us more!" Rosie wiggled her body.

"Ask yourself, in the future, what would make you feel happy, content, peaceful and satisfied, like after a good meal?" She opened her eyes and winked at her cousins. "Without feelings of regret, or doubt, or shame, without bitter taste, or tears? Let's focus on that and the best outcome we can imagine."

Mr. Guinness stared at Bailey. "Wow!" he thought. "Some wise dog!" He liked her balanced view of the problem, but he needed more. He needed a plan.

Rosie paced. Leo sat in a corner licking his paws clean.

"How about…" Miles spoke up, "creating a kiwi sanctuary? One that's safe with fencing that keeps out the stoats." Cosmo nodded approval. "That would give the kiwis peace. But where and how to do this is beyond me."

Mitch rubbed his eyes. "I'm so done, guys. Drai-ained. We gotta get up extra early tomorrow to clean up the mess. As for solving the kiwi problem? I recommend calling it quits. It's too late to make decisions, much less act upon them." The day had been very long. He expressed what they were all feeling—exhaustion, weariness in their bones and minds. "Let's talk tomorrow. We gotta sleep on this. And tonight, let's stay all together in the shed. That's okay with you, Leo?"

Leo nodded. This special evening warranted a break in his routine.

Mr. Guinness, with Mitch's help, pulled additional blankets down from hooks on the wall and laid them out on the straw. Each of the cats got a cuddly fleece: one beige, one rose and

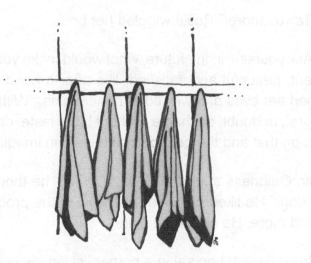

Blankets on Wall Hooks

one rust colored. Bailey and George had blankets big enough to snuggle under together. Rosie curled in close to Mr. Guinness. All were warm and safe for now, bedded down for the night.

Then Mr. Guinness realized someone was missing.

Chapter 12:
The Deep of the Night

"**W**here is Lexi?" Mr. Guinness stood up and looked around the shed.

"She must be in here somewhere," George grumbled.

"Did anyone see her after the show?" Mr. Guinness began to get alarmed. "Can someone go check the other room?"

Bailey rushed next door and rushed back. "She's not there."

"She must have gone outside to pee." Rosie lowered her voice. "Sometimes she has a tummy ache. Then she takes a little extra time."

Mr. Guinness turned to the cats. "Did you see her anywhere outside when you were up on the totara?"

"No."

Guinness's mind was racing. Was she hurt? Did the banner crash on her? Did she fall off the rocks by the stage? Did a stoat bite her? Did she get lost in the dark? Did she break a leg? Was she dog-napped? The hair on his back stood up. "Someone check outside!"

Bailey opened her eyes wide. She had never seen Mr. Guinness lose his cool like this.

"Go look outside, Bailey!" Mr. Guinness clenched his teeth. "Check around the stage! Check the hill! Check the barn! I know it's dark, but, please, go! Please!"

Bailey ran outside. They heard her call for Lexi. Silence. She called again. Again and again. Silence. After a while, she came back alone, with sad eyes, drooped ears, and dread stamped on her face. Her mouth quivered. She bit her lip. "No Lexi," she said.

"Lexi!" Rosie wailed. "I love Lexi. I should not have teased her about the TV. I was just having fun." Tears streamed down her face. "What got into me? We were having the adventure of a lifetime! How mean of me!" She dashed outside and shouted, "Lexi! LEXI! **LEXI!** Where are you?"

There was no answer, only the swoosh of the totaras in the breeze.

With her head hanging low, Rosie came back inside. "My best buddy is gone!" She thudded her face on the floor. "Do you think she's lost forever?"

Bailey put her paw on Rosie's back and stroked her gently. "My dear Rosie, regret is awful. It gnaws at the soul," she said. "But it's not too late to make it right. And you will make it right with Lexi when she is back."

"What if she doesn't come back?" Rosie sobbed.

George could not stand feeling wretched any longer. He howled so loud, the walls of the shed shook. That gave him some relief. "I'm going to look for her, right now. Who's coming with me?" He charged toward the door, but Mitch blocked his way.

"Not now, George! No! I've just made the rounds. She's not on the farm. Going out now could be dangerous. The weather may not hold. This time of the year we can have fog so dense you can't see more than one foot ahead of you." He spoke calmly, hoping reason would rein George in. If not, Mitch had other means of stopping him. Every day he managed rams, young and old. Once he even took on a cougar to save a lamb. By golly! He could deal with George.

George howled in protest.

"Listen, George!" Mitch admonished. "You are a fabulous tracker and a stellar smeller. But New Zealand is a big place. There is always risk, both from above and below. We don't want any more trouble tonight." He exchanged glances with Mr. Guinness. "We don't know what the stoats are up to," Mitch warned. "You can go look for Lexi early tomorrow. But no one is leaving tonight! Not now! Absolutely not!" Mitch closed the door. He was not to be opposed. By anyone.

George ran out of steam. No more desire to argue. He felt so tired, that he passed out on the spot. Jet lag attack! Again!

Throughout the ruckus, the three cats sat together calmly. They were not distraught. No pacing. No biting their claws. Had they no concern for Lexi? Why weren't they eager to get out and search for her? Their favorite time was the night. Venturing out in the dark was big fun—scaring opossums, killing rats and drinking their blood. Why were they just demurely whispering into each other's ears?

"How are you all so calm?" Mr. Guinness confronted them. "Do you know where she is?"

Leo did not know where Lexi was, but he had a sixth sense that she was safe. *"She'll be right, mate."* He purred, exuding comfort.

"She'll be right?" Mr. Guinness's eyes lit up. Bailey, at his side, pricked up her ears.

"I bet she's with the kiwis," Leo replied.

"With the kiwis?" Mr. Guinness wrinkled his brow. "How would she even know where they are? How would she get to them?"

"She asked me last night where they lived. I pointed in their direction." Leo yanked his head to the west, to the totara grove. "I bet she went for a bush walk in the moonlight. I bet she's having an adventure. She's got lion in her."

"She wanted to see the kiwis?" asked Mr. Guinness.

"Yeah," Leo was quick to add, "and know that they were alright."

Rosie wiped away a tear and sniffled. "That's so like Lexi. Always caring."

"Listen up, guys!" Mitch puffed out his cheeks and exhaled. He was at the end of his energy. "I've got to work tomorrow. We need to call it a day. What about you, Leo?"

Leo nodded. "We'll stay in tonight and take action in the morning." His cool New Zealand temperament showed—he just kept calm and carried on.

Young Totara—
Podocarpus totara

148

Mitch and the cousins collapsed onto their blankets. They settled down to go to sleep. Everyone except Rosie.

"Bailey!" Rosie fretted. "I'm still worried."

"When we have a problem at home," Bailey mumbled, "sometimes our family says a prayer."

"What's that?" Rosie asked.

"It's when you sit down, put your paws together, close your eyes and stay silent like meditating. It's a way to deal with chaos. I've seen it done."

"Does it work?" Rosie asked.

"It might," said Bailey.

"Will it bring back Lexi?"

"I don't know," Bailey said gently. "But if we wish for it really, really hard, and hope with all our heart, we may have good news in the morning. Come cuddle with me."

Rosie curled up, squeezed her paws together and closed her eyes. Eventually, she fell asleep. George was snoring. Mr. Guinness had rolled over on his side. Mitch was under his cover, his eyes still open. The cats, too, were still awake.

"I changed my mind," Leo whispered. "I'll go and look for her."

Mitch nodded.

"You want us to come along?" Miles asked Leo.

"I better go alone." Leo vanished out the door.

꩜꩜ Chapter 13: Walk-Ins ꩜꩜

As soon as he woke up the next morning, George announced, "I'm going to look for Lexi." He nudged Bailey, who was half-awake and barked to rouse Mr. Guinness, Rosie and the cats. Their hosts had already gone to work. Today's task was to scout for their missing sweetheart. Well, but not before having something to eat.

"It would be unwise to head out to find her, if we are weak from hunger on empty stomachs. We may need a lot of stamina today." George was sure.

While devouring breakfast, he sneezed. He raised his head to the half-cracked window and sneezed again. "What's that smell?" He sniffed, sniffled, and snorted. "That's the scent of the ocean."

How could he smell the sea so far inland? Granted, he was on the other side of the world where fall was spring, where there was no Thanksgiving and the English was weird. Was the farmer's wife bringing a fish special? He could always make room for more breakfast.

"Awk." There was a new sound! "Awk, awk." It persisted, accompanied by soft squawks.

"What's that noise?" Miles perked up. His hunting instinct kicked in. "Is that an injured bird?"

"Awk!" The sound moved closer.

"I'll check it out." George barreled through the door. He was only gone a moment before he stuck his head back in. "Guys! You better come quick! You've never seen anything like *this* before!" He produced a short yodel. "You'll never guess who is outside. They have flippers! They walk in a straight line! And they are blue!"

He darted back out. Everyone followed.

There were three of them, each one about a foot tall. They had small heads, black beaks, white chests, and their backs were blue—blue like the sea. They walked upright on two pink feet webbed in black, with a slight forward stoop. They halted and stood in front of the stunned cousins.

"What on earth?" George was sitting on the grass, in the sun, cracking up.

Cosmo whispered to Miles. "Woah! These creatures are blue like blueberries! They look like aliens."

"*Extraordinaire*, but not extraterrestrial!" Miles replied.

"How do you know they are *not* from outer space?!" Cosmo kept his voice down.

Miles shrugged his shoulders. "*Je ne sais pas.* Perhaps you are right. Maybe they *are* aliens."

The creature in the middle stepped forward daintily.

"My name is Penguin," he burbled. "Peter Penguin." With his right flipper he gestured to the creature next to him. "This is Paula Penguin, my nest neighbor." And turning to his other side, he said, "This is Paul Penguin, my bodyguard. He insisted on coming."

The cousins moved closer and stared, but George remained on the grass, still snickering and chortling without composure.

Paul, the bodyguard, walked toward George, who was five times his size. Unintimidated, his eyes wide open and unblinking, Paul gurgled at George and gestured with his flippers. George got up, slightly startled, stepped back just a bit and farted.

"Cool it." Bailey cautioned George to behave. "They may be friends of our hosts."

Mr. Guinness swallowed. "Welcome!" he said. "My name is Mr. Guinness; Guinny for short. These are my cousins. We are out of town guests." He introduced each of them.

"I beg your pardon." Peter Penguin swished the words in his mouth. "Excuse the intrusion. Normally, we don't drop in unannounced, but we've come out of dire need." He struck a pose—right foot forward, left flipper back. He pumped his chest, rolled his eyes, and pointed his bill into the air while stretching his neck high. Then he moved both flippers up and down, brayed loud, sounding like a trumpet, and waddled around in one spot. The other two penguins circled him three times with equal gusto until they all came to a standstill.

The cousins retreated a step or two and stared in wonderment at the penguins' fervor.

"May I ask where you are from?" Mr. Guinness said.

Little Blue Penguins' Display

"We come from our beach by the sea. We walked through the night."

"What a journey!" Bailey spoke up. "You must be hungry after such a long march. What can we offer you?" She suddenly realized she had no idea what penguins ate. Slightly nervous, she made eye contact with Rosie and the cats. Would they help with procuring a light meal? George would be useless in this situation; anything he found for the penguins, he would probably eat himself.

Peter Penguin waved his right flipper. "We are not hungry, but thank you. Last night we had a big dinner of squid, sprat, sardines, anchovy, krill and cod. All freshly caught. But, we would like to have some water, please."

"Of course, though we only have fresh water," Bailey said. "Do you prefer it salty?"

"It's no problem," Peter said. "We drink both."

"Follow me, please." Bailey walked toward the water buckets. The penguins paraded after her in a straight line. Mr. Guinness was impressed Bailey took the initiative. She had become quite a support dog.

While Peter, Paula and Paul slurped their fill, Bailey said, "You must be here to see Mitch and Leo. Right now they are at work."

"Yes," Mr. Guinness picked up Bailey's lead, "but they'll be back later. They did not say when. You are welcome to wait here with us. Though, if you came for the sheep shearing show, I believe you are out of luck. You may want to try back in a month or two."

"We came to see you, specifically," Peter Penguin replied.

"Me?"

"You and your troupe."

"Us?" Mr. Guinness asked.

"We applaud you on your performance last night," gushed Peter Penguin. "Even if the show, uh, ended early."

Mr. Guinness's eyes opened wide in surprise. "How do you know about that?"

"The albatrosses were raving about your show all night. We birds are connected. We know what's going on." Peter Penguin swished the words in his mouth. "We are fascinated by what you did."

"You are?"

"I wish we could have been here," Peter Penguin continued.

"You do?"

"Yes. We penguins love shows."

Mr. Guinness scooted closer. "How do you know about shows?"

"Our friends, the humpback whales, are singer/songwriters. We attend their gigs all the time. They compose beautiful melodies with whistles and rumbles, with groans, moans and clicks, with crescendos and codas. For their grand finales they leap from the depths of the sea into the air, slapping their massive flippers and spouting geysers from their blowholes." Peter Penguin's words flowed. "When they crash back into the water, their splashes are spectacular. You should see them in the moonlight. We invite you to come and watch from our beach!"

"That sounds dramatic." Mr. Guinness liked this tiny creature's vigor and passion. "We'd be happy to talk about show business, but can it wait just a bit?" He did not want to be rude, but he too was anxious to get Lexi back. He did not want to waste a moment or delay George's quest to find her. "We have a troupe member missing and we must get her back."

Humpback Whale Tail #1—
Megaptera novaeangliae

Humpback Whale Tail #2

Humpback Whale Tail #3

"So very sorry." Peter Penguin bowed and stepped back. "Our troubles must wait."

"When *are* you going to look for Lexi?" Rosie whimpered to George. "*When?*"

"Give him a minute," Bailey pleaded under her breath.

"Troubles?" The penguins stepped forward. "Is there anything we can do to help?"

Mr. Guinness felt his tummy getting warm. He really liked these guys. They were so very polite. "Our time here is limited," he said. "We don't know how much longer we can stay. Please, tell me why you've come to see us. You came a long way. And we know what it is to travel a great distance."

"Thank you," Peter began. "Our mission is urgent—a matter of life and death. Our survival depends on you helping us."

Mr. Guinness gasped. Mission? Life and death? Where was this going?

Peter paused and spread his flippers, to include his buddies in his speech. "I'm speaking for all the penguins of this island— the erect-crested, the Fjordlands, the snares, the yellow-eyed penguins and the rockhoppers." He shifted uneasily from foot to foot. "We, the blue penguins, are the smallest and we have the biggest problem. Our rookery appointed me to come talk with you."

"What is the problem?" Mr. Guinness raised a brow.

"These vermin who ruined your show last night! The stoats!" Peter burbled. "They invade our nests. They slurp our eggs and eat our chicks. Paula has lost three eggs. Three! Devoured! Gone! Forever! She is devastated." Peter sloshed around on his feet. "It was Paula who first proposed to meet with you."

Paula wiped away tears with her flipper as the cousins moved closer.

"The stoats attack you too?" Rosie asked, her eyes huge.

Bailey's eyes welled. "I feel so sorry for you all."

"Something *must* be done." Peter Penguin stretched his chest to expose his full size. "It is urgent. Something needs to happen right now, but we just don't know what." He opened his flippers and stood still for a moment, in silence, then raised his voice. "Our kind has been on this earth for forty million years. We want to survive. We want to live. The abuse by the stoats must end!"

Mr. Guinness's eyes were aglow. The penguins were asking for more than raising awareness. They were asking to be saved. This *was* a matter of life and death. "How can we help?"

George positioned himself in front of all of them, accommodating his belly between his hind legs. "War!" he blurted out. "I said it last night! No question! All-out war!"

Mr. Guinness frowned. Bailey scratched behind her ear.

"We cats know how to kill," Miles offered. "We kill mice all the time." Cosmo nodded solemnly. "But we kill to eat. What you are talking about is different. War! *La guerre!* Not our thing! *Non! Absolument!*"

"We came to New Zealand as artists, not as warriors," Cosmo added. "We didn't come to fight stoats. No frickin way."

"What can we do?" Bailey asked. "What is realistic?"

"We set a trap." George's face flushed. "We dig a trench. We camouflage it with stuff from around here, and wait. They all will fall in."

"And then what?" Mr. Guinness asked.

"Kill them! Of course." George was matter-of-fact about it.

Mr. Guinness shook his head. "Violence does *not* work in the long run. We need a plan where everyone wins. The kiwis, the penguins, and the stoats. We need to play the long game." He cradled his head in his paws. What a challenge!

Peter Penguin softened his tone. "George, we appreciate your enthusiasm, but for us, it's not about war or killing the stoats. We just want to be left alone. We know how to out-maneuver sea lions when they block our nests. We fight petrels, seagulls and skuas who pray on our chicks. As painful as it can be, we know there's a natural cycle of life and death. It's part of our reality, but what the stoats are doing is different."

Paula gave George a long sorrowful look. "The stoats are reckless," she spoke from experience. "They are devastating. They are out of sync with our world. They are destroying its natural balance. We need a long-term solution."

Peter put his flipper around Paula.

"How about this?" George began again. "We mark a border with our pee around the place where the kiwis and where all of you penguins live. Everybody can help. That would nauseate the stoats and drive them off." George absolutely believed in the power of bodily production.

"Could that actually work?" asked Mr. Guinness. He was a bit incredulous.

"Stoats probably love stinky smells." Rosie suggested snidely.

Bailey lowered her eyes. "And what if it rains?"

"If we could work on insight ..." Mr. Guinness paused, hoping for inspiration. "Insight into the consequences of their behavior, or if we could get them to understand somehow? Any ideas? Miles? Cosmo?" He wished Mitch and Leo would come home to brainstorm with them. After all, this was a local matter.

Suddenly, bellbirds, tuis and kakas started chirping. Loud chatter came from the young totara bushes. Tweeting, twitting and twittering filled the air. The sentinels of the forest rang out. The bird sound system had been activated. Crescendo! There was movement in the underbrush. All eyes turned to the west. What was going on?

Nose up, ears erect, mane in the wind, Lexi emerged. Her collar jingled. Her fur was matted with burrs but her step was brisk.

Leo strutted behind her through the open gate and into the compound. "Guess where I found her!" he yelled. He threw up his paws. "You'll never believe it!"

"I'm back," Lexi said triumphantly, grinning all over her little face. "I've met the stoats, and they are not all bad."

◎/◎ Chapter 14: Relief ◎/◎

Everyone rushed over to Lexi. Rosie somersaulted. George roared with joy, howling at full throttle. Bailey barked with happiness. Mr. Guinness smiled, his heart filled with thanks. They swarmed Lexi and snuggled her. They licked her face, her back, her tail and her belly. The cats, being a bit more restrained, grinned at the scene.

Lexi loved her cousins' affection—she kissed them right back. She had a scratch on her nose and her hair was tangled, but her smile was radiant: proof that her adventure, whatever it had been, had been worth it.

"What happened to you?" Mr. Guinness burned with curiosity.

"We-ell," Lexi flirted with a New Zealand accent. "Let me tell you!" She took a deep breath. "While we were waiting to perform the pantomime, I started getting into character and feeling the story. I was so sad for the kiwis that my stomach hurt. I really, really wanted to tell them they should not despair. Then the banner suddenly crashed down and everything went nuts. I was so distressed, I decided to find them. I headed to the grove where Leo said they lived. On the way, I came across these creatures—these youngsters. I knew they were not kiwis, because they were furry and walked on four legs. They cheered me along in the moonlight and I wasn't sure I knew where to go. I felt kind of lost, but they invited me to come with them to their home. So, I said 'yes.'"

"Who were they?" Mr. Guinness asked.

"Stoats."

"Stoats?" George blurted out. "No way!"

"Yes. Stoats!" Lexi's eyes glowed. "They were so cute! So nice! So likable! They led me through a maze of underbrush and I squeezed through the gaps in the thicket. When we got to their camp, I met their daddy."

"You're kidding!" Rosie snickered. "Lexi! You *are* making this up! You got lost in the woods and you are lucky that Leo found you."

"No, Rosie!" Lexi stomped her foot. "I went there. I had to go because..."

"Because why?" The little grey terrier was impatient to learn the details.

"Because I thought..."

"Yes?" interrupted Rosie, but then she stopped herself. She really was happy to have Lexi back. She continued gently. "Lexi, what did you think you could do?"

"Well, I thought I could make a difference." Lexi sat down and held her head high. "At least try to make a difference. I wanted to do some good."

"So lovely, Lexi." Bailey smiled.

"Their daddy's name is Sam. The girl stoats call him Sam the Savage; the boys call him Sam the Sage."

All the cousins sat still, somber and silent. Lexi had their full attention.

"Sam asked what I was doing in their camp and what we were doing on their island. He knew all about all of us visiting—like he had been spying on us. He said we should get lost, because it's none of our business what goes on in New Zealand."

"What did you say?" Bailey asked wide-eyed.

"Well, I was holding my breath because the camp was really smelly."

"I knew they'd stink," Rosie interrupted. "In more than one way."

"But what did you say?" Bailey insisted.

"The stench bothered me," Lexi admitted, "but I just went for it. Once I started talking, it all came out in one big pile of words and I just kept going. I said to Sam, 'Hello, Sir. I'm Lexi and I'm from California and the hummingbirds told us we needed to come to New Zealand. They said we could help save the kiwis. And then we learned from the sheep that the problem was with the stoats. That's you guys. And that the stoats were killing the kiwis. And if the stoats kill the kiwis of New Zealand, there won't be any left anywhere anymore. And Mr. Sam, Sir, do you want to be known as a killer? Is that your legacy?' That's what I said. And then I had to take another deep breath, and it did really stink there, but I kept talking. I realized I was talking louder and louder, and a whole group of stoats had gathered around and was listening. 'Sir, I'm asking for your help,' I said. 'We came half way around the world to help the kiwis. With respect, Sir! Please, think about it.'"

"You said all that?" Rosie was skeptical.

"Were you not afraid?" Bailey said with eyes wide open, her brows and ears raised. George chortled in the background.

"I was nervous, but I shook my mane and stretched my chest and stood up on my hind legs in front of Sam and his clan. I pretended that I was strong." Lexi giggled.

"You blow me away," Mr. Guinness confessed. He sat back on his hunches and beamed with pride.

"I really could not stop talking once I got started. I asked Sam if he realized the effect of their appetite. He frowned and got really defensive, snarling 'No, no, no,' but I would not let up. 'How about your baby stoats?' I said. 'Would you like for them to be eaten, devoured and killed? If you could change your family's eating habits just a little bit, you might gain the respect of all New Zealand.'"

"How did you come up with all this?" Rosie's voice cracked with incredulity.

"I figured he loved his kids. Doesn't every parent love their kids? And I said that if I had babies, I'd be sad if they all got eaten. And wouldn't a stoat be sad about that too? Sam's clan listened."

"*Incroyable! Quel courage!*" Miles shouted.

"*Quel cœur!*" Cosmo seconded.

"And how did Sam respond to all that?" Mr. Guinness needed to know.

"He spit on the ground and pranced in front of his folks in the moonlight. There were a lot of them. A LOT of stoats! They watched him strutting around and around, but they kept quiet."

"Did he seem threatening?" Mr. Guinness asked.

"Not at all! He wrinkled his face, like he was thinking really hard. I figured I had come so far, I might as well go all the way. So I told Sam he has the power to tell his clan not to eat kiwi chicks and kiwi eggs and to just leave them alone. And that's not all."

"There is more?!" Rosie asked.

Lexi cleared her throat. "I told him how impolite it was to disturb our show, and he grinned. I made it very clear it was not funny. I told him how hard we had worked on it and how much we wanted to entertain. And then he asked, and he seemed a bit hurt when he asked," Lexi paused for dramatic effect, "he asked, 'How come we were not invited?' That took me by surprise, but I did not let him see that. Instead, I told him I was very sorry that we did not reach out. And I left it at that."

"And then what?" Mr. Guinness could not get enough. His tail was wagging so fast that he accidentally knocked Rosie over.

"He said he would see what he could do. He also wondered why no one ever talked to him about the problem. They should have come to him. I think he wants to improve his image, get a public relations makeover. I learned that expression from watching TV." Lexi looked at Rosie and smiled. "They took really good care of me. Sam offered me a termite treat, but I told him 'no thank you,' because I was a vegetarian. He had never heard of that. When I explained it, he laughed his head off. Then I told him I thought stoats could eat veggies too, and also berries. He laughed even harder. Definitely, they could eat slugs and worms. He nodded to that. Then, he asked if I wanted to spend the night and I accepted. And when I woke up, Leo walked in. The stoats seemed to know him, but they kept their distance. And that's my story."

"Wow!" George got up to stretch his legs. "Wow! Wow! Wow! When our Lexi is on a roll, watch out world!"

Termites—*Isoptera*

"This little one was a hero last night," Leo said. "Shall we call her Lexi Lion Heart?"

Mr. Guinness hi-fived Leo as everyone nodded.

Lexi was having the time of her life. What she accomplished gave her such feelings of reward. And it felt so good to be with her family.

"And now that we have her back, we can go home."

"Who said that?" Mr. Guinness frowned. He looked each cousin in the eyes.

"I did." Miles stepped forward. "And I will say it again!" The others pretended they had not heard him and embraced Lexi some more. "Cosmo and I believe we should contact Condor and get out of here."

Mr. Guinness pressed his lips together. He did not like what he was hearing, but he understood.

"My dear Miles and Cosmo," he said rather formally, "You really want to leave now? It seems there is still a chance to make things better here."

"I'm telling you, the stoats are not all bad." Lexi was sure.

"Give us one more day," Mr. Guinness pleaded with the cats.

"Just one more day!" Leo said, putting one foot forward in a gesture of encouragement.

Miles and Cosmo stared at Leo who exuded confidence, his paws on his hips. They felt a kinship to Leo, not only because they were fellow cats, but because they had collaborated. They had worked together as artists.

"How can you be so cavalier?" Cosmo asked Leo.

"I suppose, I'm just a cavalier cat." Leo grinned. "Let's see what we can do with one more day. Make a big difference, maybe?" He thought, "These foreigners! They are so amusing."

The Hollywood cats nodded reluctantly. "Okay."

Mr. Guinness exhaled. "Thank you, Leo." He nodded to the penguins by the water buckets. "We must work out something that gives *them* and the kiwis hope."

"Who are *they*?" Lexi whispered. "In my excitement, I didn't even see them." Mr. Guinness extended his paw.

"Lexi and Leo," he said, "may I introduce our new penguin friends, Peter, Paul and Paula?" He motioned to the trio. "They have come to us for help. Just like the kiwis, they face extinction by the stoats."

Lexi walked over to greet them. "So glad to meet you, Peter, Paul, Paula, though I'm so sorry we are meeting under such unfortunate circumstances." She had never before encountered so many new creatures, much less in one day. What else was possible? Looking at the penguins and their shiny coat, Lexi decided that blue was her favorite color.

The penguins bowed. Peter asked, "You really spoke with the stoats? I'm amazed they are capable of conversation. We only know them as killers."

"And the stoats don't really know you yet," added Lexi.

"We must somehow find a middle ground." Mr. Guinness wrinkled his brow.

"I have an idea." Lexi shook her mane. "The young stoats don't really like Sam that much. They told me that he and the aunts and uncles and grandparents are old, bossy fogies. *They* are the ones eating kiwi eggs and chicks. One itty bitty stoat told me she hated the kiwi eggs her father makes her eat. They tasted icky, yucky and too salty. And the smell! She and her buddies prefer slimy slugs and crunchy cockroaches." Lexi stepped forward, "Maybe penguin eggs are too fishy for young stoats. If we impress on everyone *how very* fishy they are....." Suddenly her eyes got large and panic spread over her face. "Oh!" she said, "I don't mean to offend you," she addressed Peter, Paul and Paula. "I'm just saying..."

The penguins awked. "No problem. None at all. Go on, please!"

"I don't like fish myself," Lexi said pursing her little mouth in apology. "I don't like eating any animals, fish or otherwise. If we make it clear to the young stoats that it's bad to eat penguin eggs, maybe that's the way to go. I don't believe the stoats mean to be mean. Maybe the stoats could even meet the kiwis and penguins?" She paused to take a sip from the water buckets. "Maybe we could all learn to get along?"

"It's worth a try," Mr. Guinness was positive. "Shall we give diplomacy a chance?"

"I still say we need to kill the stoats," George said. He broke wind, loudly, and he burped.

"Diplo- what?" Lexi asked.

"Diplomacy," Mr. Guinness replied.

"It's when you talk politely to work things out. You talk instead of fighting. You talk instead of going to war," Rosie explained.

"Yes," Bailey agreed. "War should be a thing of the past. Killing out of hatred and ignorance sours the soul. It's time to try something new." Bailey's inclinations tended toward the positive. She turned to George. "We can do better. We must find a compromise."

"You and your big words!" George frowned.

"You know about compromise, George. You made a compromise when you agreed to come to New Zealand after insisting on going to Africa. Compromise means we talk, listen and find common ground. Maybe you don't get everything you want, but you find a way forward. A way forward without violence." George stared at her for a moment, then hiked over to the water buckets. He had to think this one over.

"You guys are nuts!" Rosie was blunt. "Lexi talking to Sam last night was one thing. But talk is cheap. How naïve can you be? Stoats are mean creatures. They are bad by nature. They proved that when they ruined our show."

"No one is all bad," Lexi insisted.

"No, Lexi," Rosie objected, shaking all over. "You are dead wrong! Some are *all* bad."

"Have you ever met a stoat, Rosie?" Lexi stared at her defiantly.

"No."

"Have you ever talked to a stoat?" Lexi insisted.

"No."

"Have you ever spent the night in a stoat camp like I have?"

"No."

"So how would you know if the stoats are all bad?" Lexi finished. Rosie may be well-read, but that did not mean she knew everything. It was Lexi's turn to teach Rosie something new.

"Remember the people that abandoned us on the street?" Rosie replied in a small voice. "They were all bad."

"Their action at the time was bad," Lexi said. "But who says they can't learn? Everyone can learn. Everyone can better themselves. We bettered ourselves, didn't we? Like when we conquered our fears and came to New Zealand."

"You are in denial." Rosie shook her head. "Bad is bad."

"No, Rosie! No!" Lexi replied. "We change all the time. Everyone does. We all can change for the better."

"Do not forget the evil deeds!" Rosie insisted and began pacing.

"Rosie!" Lexi raised her voice. "I don't want to *forget*. I want to *forgive*."

Rosie stopped. She stared at the grass.

"What if they saw us now, I mean the people that dumped us," Lexi said. "They would probably want us back."

"Would you go back?" Rosie asked.

"No. I'd throw them a kiss and move on."

"What? Just like that?"

"Yes. Just like that. I don't want the past to make me sad. How can I move forward with joy, if I always worry about what's already happened? I don't want to stumble over rocks behind me. I can't change the past, but I can change how I think about it."

Rosie could not believe what she was hearing. Was this the same Lexi she knew from California? Stunned, she stayed silent.

"Ladies," Mr. Guinness joined them. "I believe this approach is promising." He turned to the cats. "Miles and Cosmo, I know you want to go home, but would you please consider staying another day?"

Miles looked at Cosmo. Neither cat wanted this trip to end on a bad note. "We came with you to New Zealand to be artists, to perform, to do something sublime. Together. And we will stick together now. We will stay one more day. We agreed, didn't we, *mon ami*?"

Cosmo did not respond. He raised his head and stared into the eastern sky.

"You hear that?" he asked. Cats' ears were incredibly sharp. "Could it be..." Cosmo locked eyes with Miles. "The Condors?"

"Oh no! Not yet!" Mr. Guinness's eyes flickered in panic. "It can't be time to go already. We are starting to get somewhere. We are not ready to leave. Our work isn't done here. Our mission is not yet accomplished."

"It's time to pack our things," Miles said matter-of-factly.

⊙⊙ Chapter 15: The Idea ⊙⊙

The sky darkened as a giant creature appeared and landed with a powerful swoosh. It was Condor Chiara. The cousins ran to greet her.

"If she is flying solo, without her squadron, I'm not going," Cosmo hissed to Miles. "No frickin' way!"

Mr. Guinness overheard and ignored Cosmo's remark. "Chiara! I'm happy to see you. However, we are not yet ready to leave. We need more time to finish our mission. And actually..." He lowered his eyes and his voice, "we could use some help."

"That is why I am here," Condor Chiara said. "I have brought you what you need, or rather *who* you need."

Out of her down-lined basket jumped a jet-black dog with tan paws, honey colored spots over her eyes and a gray muzzle. Though advanced in years, she had a slender, muscular body, and her tail wagged in excitement.

"Aunt Jetta? What a surprise!" Mr. Guinness extended his front paws in welcome. "So wonderful to see you!"

Rosie and Lexi covered Aunt Jetta with kisses. Bailey and George cheered. The cats purred intensely.

"Hello, everyone!" she said. "I'm so glad to be here. It's so very good to see you all."

Aunt Jetta was a blue heeler, a working breed known for herding sheep and cattle, but she had been a house pet all of her life. She lived in that woodsy Midwest town of Parkville in Missouri where the cousins had their first performance. She had helped organize their smashing success.

"How are things at home?" Lexi wanted to know.

"I have good news," Aunt Jetta's eyes sparkled. "I bring greetings from Harvey."

"Harvey? The duck? But he is dead!" Lexi raised her right paw over her eyes and teared up. "The coyotes killed him when he ushered them to their seats. They were wicked and ate him." Lexi began reliving the shock she and her cousins had gone through, the grief they had felt.

"Well, that's what we all thought. But he survived and came back. He was weak and wounded, but I nursed him back to health. Then we had a big party in his honor," Aunt Jetta wagged her tail. "Granted, he's got a big old ugly scar on one leg, where the feathers won't grow back, but he's feisty as ever, still living right next door." Her eyes shined with joy.

"How did you know we were in New Zealand?" wondered Mr. Guinness.

"Condor Chiara came to see me. She told me about your trip, your mission and said I was needed. Change had to happen, she said, and that I could help make that change." Aunt Jetta smiled at Chiara. "And she's always known that I want to do

174

more than sit by the window, guarding the house, watching the neighborhood and waiting for my family to come home."

The cousins absorbed the news with wide eyes and wagging tails.

"I asked Condor if time was of the essence. She said it was. So I hopped on board," Aunt Jetta winked. "And here I am."

"Right on!" George grinned. He liked action. He liked doing things.

Condor stepped back from the group and stretched her wings. "I will check back with you tomorrow evening. Be the change you want to see. I wish you well. Stay true to your intentions." She turned into the breeze and lifted off. The cousins followed Chiara with their eyes as she ascended into the sky.

Mr. Guinness embraced Aunt Jetta. "It really is so good to see you, my dear. Are you tired?"

"I rested on the flight over. Let's get going on this mission to save the kiwis," Aunt Jetta was inspired. "I've been thinking about this the whole flight and I have an idea, Guinny. Can I run it by you first? In private?"

"Of course." He escorted her into the shearing shed and closed the door. He led her up onto the turquoise stage.

Aunt Jetta stood at the railing and took a moment to look around. The sight of the folded colored fleeces and the scent of wool and lanolin felt strangely familiar. She had the feeling she had experienced this before, but she did not know how or when or why. She closed her eyes and inhaled deeply. A warm sensation came over her, like she was finally home.

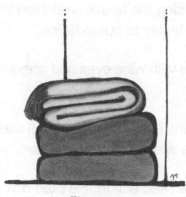

Fleeces

Mr. Guinness cleared his throat. "May I hear your idea?"

Aunt Jetta opened her eyes and smiled. "Yes, Guinny. I have come to start a school."

"A what?"

"A school. A stoat school."

Mr. Guinness sat down in front of her. "A school? Why a school?"

"Non-violence is the only way to a better future for all of us. We can teach young stoats to be respectful and to change their destructive behavior. It's never been done before, but it's worth a try. Trust me," Aunt Jetta said. "We have no time to waste."

"I like your idea," he said and paused for a moment. "But the threat is larger than we thought. It's not just about the kiwis. Another group is involved—the little blue penguins are also endangered."

Aunt Jetta smiled. "The principle of non-violence is universal. It applies—whether it's to save the kiwis or the blue penguins or both. We will address it all." She headed down the stage steps. "Shall we tell the cousins?"

Mr. Guinness followed and stopped her at the door. "Just one second! If you do not mind, I prefer *you* telling them about this approach. You have my full support, but I have no idea how to even begin." Mr. Guinness knew his troupe could be boisterous and opinionated—unpredictable. He did not know what their response would be. "Will you take the lead and organize the effort? Help us to learn how to help?"

"Guinny," she said. "Relax! That's why I'm here."

Outside, everyone was getting restless. Rosie walked around in circles. Lexi scratched her belly. George pawed at the grass, and Bailey was hoping George would not make a hole they'd have to fill in later. The cats practiced French and Maori vocabulary by the water buckets, where the penguins pranced about on their webbed feet.

Mr. Guinness opened the door with a flourish. "Cousins! Friends! Aunt Jetta has come with an idea, a really fascinating idea. Come closer, so you can hear. Prepare to be amazed! She will be pitching a brand new concept. I ask that we all hear her out," and he locked eyes with George, "before we comment. Aunt Jetta," he turned to her and bowed, "the meadow is yours."

"My dear family," Aunt Jetta began. "I believe we should start a school for the stoats, where we *teach* them to stay away from kiwis, penguins and their eggs." She looked compassionately at Peter, Paul and Paula. "We will broaden the stoats' minds and educate them to develop new appetites more in harmony with their environment. We want to change the stoats' behavior with education, not with force."

The penguins waddled closer.

"Did you say you'll teach them?" Peter Penguin asked leaning forward. "Teach them that our nests are off limits?"

"Yes," Aunt Jetta said.

"What a brilliant idea! Yes! Yes! Yes!" Paula twirled her flippers as Peter high-fived his body guard.

"Aunt Jetta!" George bellowed. "We love you, but this is c-r-a-z-y! Teach the stoats?" He laughed so hard he began to cough.

"Yes, George." Aunt Jetta was unperturbed. "Teach them to stay away from kiwis and penguins."

George stomped the ground. "You've got it all wrong! We've got to fight the bastards. I say, corral 'em, corner 'em and kill them."

"Kill them?" Lexi cried. "No! They have become my friends!"

"George!" Aunt Jetta sat right in front of him, ignoring the cloud of spittle and fug he produced with his words. "We will NOT engage in violence. No!" She raised her voice for everyone to hear. "War is an unpredictable, uncontrollable beast. War is ugly. It brings out the worst in creatures. The outcome is unknowable and both sides get hurt. There is another way."

"Listen to Aunt Jetta, George!" Bailey chimed in. "Imagine if it works!" She yearned for George's sense of conviviality, camaraderie and fairness to appear.

"Bailey, you sound like Aunt Jetta. Are you two in cahoots?" George was suspicious. "What's going on here?"

The penguins awked and waddled around the group. Peter Penguin spoke up, "If I may say, our relatives, the rockhoppers, may be of assistance. They are known to be great teachers."

"Fantastic!" Aunt Jetta was thrilled. "I'd love to meet them. The more we can involve the community, the better. And we can use all the help we can get."

Miles and Cosmo cradled their faces. They moaned. They fell flat on their bellies and buried their heads under their paws.

"Cousins! Do you know what you are asking?" Miles lifted his head and peeked out. "Establishing a school is one thing, but how are you going to get the stoats to come?" He pulled himself up. "How will you convince them to attend school of their own free will? You are dreaming." He shook his head knowingly. "And even if they came... We artists learn new things all the time. But stoats? Can stoats learn? Can they be educated? Really? Guys!? Come on!"

"What if you are wrong, Miles?" Lexi raised her voice to be heard. "I'm sure stoats can learn. Anyone can learn." She rubbed her paws in anticipation. "And, maybe, there are stoat artists, too."

Miles looked at her in wonderment.

"How do we know, if we don't try?" Bailey joined the discussion. "I didn't know I could be an artist until someone taught me. Maybe it's the same with the stoats. Nothing ventured, nothing gained."

"It is a revolutionary idea. Think how incredible it would be if it worked." Aunt Jetta stood up and smiled. "And if it doesn't, we will figure out why and think of something else."

"This is beautiful," Bailey sat up straight. "It's about teaching respect for one another. That's a very good thing." Bailey looked at George. "The stoats can learn to respect others, the kiwis and the penguins. Just like we learned to respect the cats—isn't that right George?"

"Respect them?" George huffed. "We love them! But this is different. This school thing is outlandish! "You are all N-U-T-T-Y-nutterson!" he exclaimed.

Just then, Mitch announced his approach with rapid barks. He had been at work in the hills. Constantly vigilant, always observant and never oblivious, he had seen Condor's approach—her landing and departure. He left Angus in charge and hurried down to find out what was happening. "Don't I know that bird?" he shouted.

"Yes!" explained Mr. Guinness. "Condor Chiara! She brought us a volunteer."

Mr. Guinness presented Mitch to Aunt Jetta and Aunt Jetta to Mitch. The two sniffed noses, ears, necks and butts. They locked eyes and hit it off immediately. Both were shepherds with the same work ethic and with the same love of order and discipline. Their instincts were a match, like soulmates.

"Welcome!" Mitch said. "So pleased to meet you."

Aunt Jetta felt like he was a kindred spirit. He was her cup of water. She was his.

"The pleasure is all mine." She smiled and wagged her tail.

Mitch turned to the cousins. "You all keep on talking. Let me take care of our honored guest." He nodded to Aunt Jetta. "May I offer you food and drink? What would you like? May I give you a tour of our place?"

"Delighted," she smiled. "Thank you! I'm not picky. Anything is fine."

Mitch led her to the shearing shed. They entered through the doggie door. After presenting her with refreshments, Mitch asked her, "What brings you to our farm?"

"Condor wanted me to help out and I promised her I'd do my best. And Mitch," she continued, her eyes shining with joy. "Let me tell you how absolutely thrilled I am to be here. This is such a special place. This is my dream come true."

"Oh?" Mitch was amused. The sheep farm was his workplace and dear to him, but he did not see it as particularly special.

"I have fantasized about being on a farm all my life," she said. "I love to be useful, but my life with my family was a life of leisure. There were no sheep to herd, no lambs to protect, no work to do. I made the best of it. I practiced my skills every day, telling myself that I had to train and stay fit so that I would be ready when my time came to be useful. And I think that moment is finally here."

Mitch sat still, very amazed.

"I have perfected my turns, my back-ups, and stops. Because I knew that one day, I would do the real thing on a farm, in fresh air, in summer and winter, in snow, rain or shine, under the wide open sky. My time is now."

Mitch, the stoic shepherd, had tears welling up in his eyes. What he took for granted every day was a dream come true for her. "So you want to help with the herding?" he asked.

"It would be my absolute delight," Aunt Jetta said. "But I want to do more than that."

"More?" Mitch wiggled his body. He was smitten.

"May I take you up on your offer to tour the farm?" Aunt Jetta asked. "I will tell you all about it."

"Yes. Come with me."

⊚⊚ Chapter 16: A Risk ⊚⊚

Up in the totaras, bellbirds, magpies and black-shouldered
lapwings erupted into a cacophony of noise.

Bellbird—*Anthornis melanura*   Magpie—*Cracticus tibicen*

Black-Shouldered Lapwing—
Vanellus novahollandiae

Their ruckus was so loud it woke everyone up from their afternoon naps. The chirping became shrill. The tuis joined in, flapping their blue wings. The bird sentinels of the forest sounded the alarm. Fluttering intensified. Birds plunged from branches and, just short of hitting the ground, they swooped back up. The forest was on alert.

The cousins barked and howled in confusion.

Lexi knew the smell. That musk was unforgettable. Could it be ...?

Yes!

Sam the Stoat paraded into the compound—small ears, thick brown fur, short stout legs, and a black-tipped tail. The scent released from his butt glands heralded a bold entry. Four smaller stoats, some of the mothers Lexi had met the night before, followed close behind. She ran towards them. Sam rose up on his hind legs, exposing a white belly. He greeted her with a two-paw touch.

Lexi beamed with joy.

Abruptly, the penguins stopped preening. They barricaded themselves behind the water buckets, shivering with fear. Never had they witnessed such a scene in broad daylight.

George bared his teeth, but a sudden sneezing attack overwhelmed him. The robust pungency made his eyes tear up. Snot dripped from his nose. He had sniffed strong odors before, but this was a new challenge to his sinuses. He buried his snout in his paws.

"Uhoh... What's going to happen now?" Rosie bounced from one side to the other. "Look!" She pointed to Sam and company. "Don't *they* turn all white in the winter and become precious ermines? I've read about them." She'd seen that in a picture book on outfits of kings and queens of Europe.

As for Miles and Cosmo, they immediately raced up the nearest totara, their ears flattened in alarm. No way to tell what might come of this. *Parbleu!* Watching from a high perch was their preferred modus operandi. Leo, ever fearless, non-chalant and amused, remained sitting at the base of the totara, waiting for the scene to unfold.

Mr. Guinness Meets Sam the Stoat

The hair on Mr. Guinness's back stood up in a two-inch-wide line, like a mohawk down the length of his spine, from neck to tail. A rumble escaped his chest. As a diplomatic dog, he did not growl very often, at least not in public. But this was different. Sam, the kiwi and penguin killer, had intruded. Mr. Guinness's eyes turned red. He breathed fast and heavy. His mind was revving. Sam must have organized the attack on the night show. Why was he here now? This might not be a social call.

Bailey felt the negative emotion consuming Mr. Guinness. She rubbed against his side, hoping to soothe him, to diffuse his tension, to help him gain control. She wagged her tail in deliberate slowness. She whispered in his ear. "Talk to him! This is an opportunity." Mr. Guinness remained tense and rigid. Gingerly and, as nonchalantly as she could, she walked in front of him. That interrupted his intensity and broke his penetrating focus on Sam. Mr. Guinness had a moment to blink, to reflect and regroup.

Lexi called out. "Guinny! Come and meet Sam!"

Mr. Guinness looked at her with raised eye brows. Lexi had brought on this visit. That tiny creature was the one with all the courage. The hair on his back smoothed. His breathing calmed. He decided to play it cool. "We are civilized and we will show it," he thought. How could he use this very moment for good? Even though he despised what the stoats had done, this was a new beginning. He stepped forward.

"My name is Mr. Guinness," he said in the most neutral tone he could muster. The difference in size between him and Sam was massive. "These are my other cousins, Bailey, Rosie and George. Miles and Cosmo, our cat cousins, are up there in the tree. I believe you already know Leo." He assumed the penguins would rather not be introduced as they were still huddling behind the water buckets.

"Sam is the name," the stoat replied with a raspy voice. As he spoke, he exposed a toothy underbite with a missing incisor. "Curiosity brings me, spurred on by my new friend, that charming Lexi." He smiled, exposing a pink jaw with more missing teeth.

Rosie stopped pacing. George uncovered his face to look. The cats in the tree strained to hear.

"I needed to see for myself what's going on," said Sam. "And I came to apologize for last night. My teenagers pulled that stunt."

That stunned Mr. Guinness. He had been so quick to blame Sam for the chaos, all of it.

Bailey smiled knowingly. "Teenagers. They have minds of their own, don't they?"

Mr. Guinness took her cue. "Yes. Apology accepted." He decided to play it safe.

Mr. Guinness was aware of his audience. The penguins watched nervously, the cats were in suspense, and George was potentially a loose cannon. "I appreciate you coming." Mr. Guinness took the diplomatic road. "Shall we talk in private?" he nodded toward the shearing shed.

Sam's grin faded. "Right here is good. I prefer to speak in the open." He was weary of falling for a possible trick of canine proportions. Key to his survival and the survival of his clan was the keenness to avoid a trap.

The dog cousins stared. George kept quiet. The cats in the totara did not move. The twittering from the trees died down. Silence descended on the group.

"I'll come right to the point." Mr. Guinness seized the moment. "Kiwis and penguins are in danger of extinction. You and your clan are killing them. You threaten their survival."

"We all do what we must to survive," Sam said curtly. "No one ever has brought that up as a problem."

"It is a BIG problem," Lexi moved closer. "Once you eat them, that's it," uttered Lexi. "No more. Ever. We would like to help solve the problem. And you, Sam, can make it happen. Truly. You can make the difference. You are the key to that change."

Sam stared at her with black beady eyes.

Miles and Cosmo moved down a branch to take it all in. Leo had left his spot under the totara to sit next to Lexi. This was a matter of massive importance, not just for this sheep farm, but for the whole island. He wanted to show his solidarity.

"What Lexi is saying..." Leo stared Sam in the face without blinking, "is that you could be the solution."

Mr. Guinness threw Leo an appreciating look. He valued his support.

"The solution? I'm not sure I agree with you about the problem. Let me tell you," Sam replied. "We come from a long line, though we did not start here in New Zealand. We were brought over here on ships a long time ago, and we make the best of it. We survived. Actually, we are thriving." He turned around and winked at his females.

The stoat ladies giggled in a chorus of approval. Seeing their Sam involved with these foreign dogs *and* with the orange cat impressed and fascinated them. They never had heard their Sam talk like that. They had never witnessed a discussion of such importance. They did not know why Sam had insisted they come along, but they liked it.

The three penguins left their security zone behind the water buckets and approached cautiously. They flapped their flippers in unison.

"With respect, awk, awk, awk," Peter Penguin, with his bodyguard on one side and Paula on the other, mustered up his courage. "Would it be a problem for you if we came to stab and eat your babies in the middle of the day?"

The lady stoats gasped. Sam spat a wide arrow of saliva. "We aren't the only ones who hunt and kill." He eyed Leo.

Bailey stepped in before the discussion got more heated. "Could we all consider a new way for everyone to get along?"

"Shall we tell Sam about our idea?" Lexi asked Mr. Guinness.

"You go ahead, my dear. You continue to amaze me." He sat down.

"Our Aunt Jetta, who came to visit ..." Lexi locked eyes with Sam. "She has the idea to start a school and teach your kids how to live in harmony with kiwis and penguins."

"Harmony?" Sam sniffed.

"That just means not eating their eggs or chicks. You could still stuff yourself with other food. All kinds of food. We'll even help your young find some." She took a deep breath. "If we set up a school, would you send your kids?"

Sam stared at Lexi. "A school? They don't need schooling." He stared at Mr. Guinness. "They imitate me and their mothers to learn survival skills."

"Of course, they learn from you. And they still would." Mr. Guinness took over. "But in school, they could learn something new and they would have fun and play games."

"And if you and your ladies come to the school sometimes as well, the young ones would have your example to follow." Bailey was right at Mr. Guinness's side.

"What?" Sam demanded impatiently.

"It's only about learning not to eat kiwi and penguin eggs and chicks. Simple as that." Lexi was on a roll. "Learn to stay out of their way, and, maybe, even learn to get along. Maybe even be friends? Sam, Sir! If you help, you'd be the hero in this neighborhood—sheep, pigs, birds, kiwis and penguins will think of you as a number one class act."

"I know the sheep have been watching us," Sam said. He was reluctant to admit how much he enjoyed attention. "But since when do the pigs care?"

"Pigs are smart. They know what's going on. They come from a long line too," Leo remarked.

"They all would notice?" Sam scratched under his chin.

"Yes. You'd get recognition beyond measure!" Mr. Guinness saw an opportunity. Of course, Sam wanted to be liked, fussed over and glorified. "You'd stand out as a model of excellence! You'd have the respect of the island and be known as Sam the Great," he proclaimed and sat down, wondering if that— maybe—was over the top.

"Sam, the Great, you say? Hmm..." Sam turned to look at his gaggle of ladies who stomped the ground with excitement.

For them, Sam was already great—even though they also knew him as Sam the Sour, especially in the mornings. They were sure that he wanted to be even greater, not just for their stoat clan, but for the whole world. And there was gravy for them in this too—the school thing might relieve the monotony of their day-to-day. The four stoat ladies raised themselves up on their hind legs, bowed to Sam, turned to each other and joined paws for a little round-the-stoatsie jig.

Sam grinned. He always did what he wanted to do, but having his females' approval was a bonus. "A school, eh? Let's see how it goes. There is nothing to lose. I'll send them," he decided. "Chaperoned by my ladies, of course. Their mothers must be involved."

Mr. Guinness and Sam sealed the deal with a paw shake.

"You are doing the right thing." Lexi batted her eyes and smiled. "When shall we start?"

"Tomorrow?" Mr. Guinness looked to Sam.

Sam nodded. He whistled at his females and they retreated back to the woods from which they had come.

*****

Lexi jumped so high she almost leaped onto Rosie's back. "Victory!" she shouted.

Rosie pouted. "Will Sam ever say he is really sorry for the banner crash?"

"Oh, Rosie, don't harp on the past. He did apologize when he first arrived," Lexi said.

Peter, Paul and Paula Penguin broke out in a short display of flipper stretches, neck elongations and beak clicking. "If we may remind you," Peter said. "We do know the perfect teachers."

Mr. Guinness bent down to look the little blue penguins in the eye. "Local participation is important," he said. "Who are these teachers?"

"Our cousins, the rockhoppers, are as tall as you, Mr. Guinness," Peter said cheerfully. "They ooze authority, if I may say." Peter quickly glanced at George. "They can be here in the morning."

"We will welcome them." Mr. Guinness was optimistic. The whole thing was an experiment. Why not have rockhoppers rock this school?

"We must leave now," Peter Penguin announced. "We thank you from the bottom of our hearts." With a nod to Paula and Paul, he started the straight-line waddle back to the sea. "Goodbye." They disappeared from view.

Mr. Guinness looked around the sheep farm. He could not believe what had just happened. Good fortune was on their side. He needed a moment and excused himself for a very long private pee behind the shed.

As Mitch and Aunt Jetta came running down the hill, back from their tour, Mr. Guinness called out. "You just missed the stoats!"

"What?" Mitch shouted in disbelief. "The stoats?"

"They were here?" Aunt Jetta chimed in. "Really?"

"Ay, mate," Leo said. "They agreed to try out the school thing! They'll be back tomorrow! Go figure!"

"We are expecting the stoat students accompanied by their mothers, and the rockhopper penguins, who will help teach," Mr. Guinness said.

Mitch produced a hearty grin. "Times are a-changing." He sat down, raised his paws over his head and thanked the universe in a dramatic gesture. "Ay, mate. Now all you've gotta do is work out a pla-an. Anything is possible."

Aunt Jetta smiled and closed her eyes. She was happy to be in New Zealand. She knew that at their core, all creatures were made from the same stuff, from stardust actually—the building blocks of the universe. Life was full of grace and her visit was not a chance occurrence, but an opportunity to bring forth a whole lot of good. She was living her dream. She was about to fulfill her destiny.

"I am ready."

◎◎ Chapter 17: The Plan ◎◎

"Let's begin," Aunt Jetta positioned herself in front Mitch and Leo, the seven cousins and Angus who had come down from the hill. She hoped everyone would give their input, any kind of input, positive or negative, as long as it was constructive. Like a teacher in front of her class, she walked up and down before the ten of them, giving them time to think. They were silent.

Before Mr. Guinness could sift through his skill set for pointers on how to come up with a school curriculum, Rosie shouted out.

"I know!" She hopped up and down and began running around in circles. "You guys! I really *do* know!" Her tongue hung out. She yapped. Her eyes glowed. "I read it in a book. Whenever you have an idea and want to make a plan, you must do S.M.A.R.T." *

Lexi darted at Rosie, giving her a friendly in-the-rump bump. "Rosie!" she giggled. "You said that wrong. You don't *do* smart, you want to *be* smart. I never thought I would correct you." She was enjoying her newly found assertiveness.

* Note: see Bibliography: Drucker

"Lexi, I mean something different. When you plan a new thing, you should apply S.M.A.R.T."

"You just want to show off, Rosie. You and your brainy stuff!" Lexi pursed her lips.

"Wait a second, ladies! Easy now! I've heard about this too," said Mr. Guinness. "S.M.A.R.T. is an acronym, yes? S – M – A – R –T."

"An ACRO what?" Lexi asked.

"An acronym," Rosie explained, "that's a word made up of letters."

"Every word is made up of letters, English, French, Maori," Lexi rolled her eyes. "So?"

"Give Rosie a chance to explain!" George barked. "Listen up!"

"Yes, each letter of an acronym is the beginning of another word. It helps you memorize a concept." Rosie was pleased to have everyone's attention.

"You mean like B.F.F.?" Lexi caught on quickly.

"What's *that* now?" Rosie moaned.

No one knew.

"BFF! **B**est **F**riends **F**orever!" Lexi giggled.

"Ahh...yes! Exactly!" Mr. Guinness cradled his face in his paw, and shook his head in amusement. "So what is S.M.A.R.T.? What does it stand for? Tell us, Rosie!"

Rosie sat down, back straight, head erect, ears up. "All right!" Rosie paused and looked around at everyone. They stared at her with anticipation. Even the cats were perfectly still.

"S.M.A.R.T. So... **S**. . ." she said, "Is for Specific. Our plan cannot be vague. To make a successful plan, it must be specific. We need to know exactly what we are doing and how we are getting it done. We want to set up a school to teach stoats how to live harmoniously with kiwis and penguins. That's pretty specific, right?" Everyone nodded.

"*Spécifique!*" Miles said with his best French accent.

"S.M.A.R.T.! Now M! **M** is for Measurable," Rosie continued. "That means we should be able to measure how successful we are and if we are meeting our goals."

"Like how many students show up," Aunt Jetta interjected. "The more, the better." She liked where this was going.

"Yes!" said Rosie. "We can take attendance every day."

Leo joined the conversation. "Or we can check how many kiwi and penguin eggs hatch after the school's been going for a while. If there are more than before the school opened, we know we're on to something."

"Very specific and very scientific, Leo!" Mr. Guinness applauded.

"And *mesurable!*" Cosmo winked at Miles. "My French is getting good."

"What's **A** for?" Mr. Guinness urged.

"**A** is for Achievable. Are the goals we set for ourselves possible? Is our plan something we can actually do, or is the plan a dream?"

"With Sam on board, we are ready to go. I know we can do it together." Aunt Jetta beamed with confidence.

"And **R**?"

"**R** is for relevant." Rosie grinned.

"Relevant, as in, is the project important? Is it meaningful? Is it worthwhile?" explained Mr. Guinness.

"As they say in French," Miles added, "Is it *apropos*?"

Leo nodded knowingly. "No question about that."

"And the **T** in S.M.A.R.T. ..."

Mr. Guinness stopped Rosie by raising his paw. "**T** is for timing. I remember now."

"Right!" Rosie wiggled in delight.

"Time has two meanings here," Mr. Guinness smiled. "The project must be timely, and so must be its completion. No missing the deadline. No oversleeping. No sloughing off. No lollygagging around."

"This is perfect!" Rosie clapped. "And now we have until tomorrow to set up the school."

Lexi threw her admiring looks.

Mitch raised a brow. He had never heard anything like this in his whole life. But, hey, if S.M.A.R.T. made sense to these visitors, why not?

Miles and Cosmo sat wide-eyed, not blinking, brushing their whiskers.

Aunt Jetta sensed their doubt. "Miles? Cosmo? Any thoughts?"

"The idea of creating a school is clever." Miles spoke slowly. "And, assuming that Sam the Stoat does not back out on his promise to send his kids, assuming they actually show up, assuming they sit still and want to learn, then what? What specifically will you teach? And how?"

"Excellent point, Miles. Thank you for your candor," Aunt Jetta said and cleared her throat. She had promised Condor Chiara to help make a difference and was committed to do it. Not just try. Do. "How do we teach new behaviors? I open the subject for discussion."

George's eyes glazed over. More talk? These cousins liked to talk! He preferred action. But if words were their way to action, so be it. He wanted to play his part. He looked at Bailey. She scratched her chin. He could tell she was thinking, so he started thinking, too. He pulled in his tummy, stretched his chest and rolled his eyes. Bailey had taught him that being a team player was a smart thing to do. Smart? Yes! That other kind of smart. He jumped forward and placed himself next to Aunt Jetta. With a quickness no one expected from his rotund body, he rolled over once and shook himself into comfort. He sat down on his butt and yodeled briefly for everyone's attention.

"We'll teach howling," he proclaimed.

"What?" Mr. Guinness wrinkled a brow.

"Howling is fun education for everyone. I will teach them proper breathing and how to get the tone loud, long and lush."

"Oh, George!" Bailey smiled. "What does howling have to do with our mission? What the stoats need to learn is respect for kiwis and penguins. It's about opening the students' eyes to new way of thinking."

George stomped his right foot. "Howling is a new thing ... for them," he insisted. "Everybody could benefit from learning how to howl. Proper howling involves breath control and discipline. It builds camaraderie to sing together. It might be a new way for them to express themselves. If howling makes me happy, maybe it would make the stoats happy, too. Happy stoats are friendly stoats."

"You are special, George." Cosmo had always admired George's vocalizations. "No one howls like you."

Mitch nudged George in the side and sat down by him. "*Mate*," he began. "In my world, if I howled during the day, my sheep might run off in confusion. But hey!" Mitch continued. "We could have a night club with the stoats on every new moon, when it's dark and spooky." He winked at Leo.

"Yeah!" George grinned.

Aunt Jetta was thrilled that George was exploring possibilities. She put her paw on his shoulder. "Let's practice S.M.A.R.T. If I understand the concept, all five letters have to be checked to make a plan. Five of five. **S.**!" Aunt Jetta said. "Is learning to howl **S**pecific? Yes it is!"

George grinned. "One down, four to go."

"But is it **S**pecific to the project?" Miles whispered. George did not hear that.

"Is it **M**easurable?" Aunt Jetta asked.

"We can measure how long and how often one howls," Rosie said. "But does it serve the school's mission? That's murky."

"Well, Rosie, let's find out. Exploring George's suggestion of howling classes using S.M.A.R.T. should clear up any murkiness. Let's keep going." Aunt Jetta said. "How about **A**chievable? George, can you be the howling coach, who teaches here every school day?"

"No, I can't," George admitted. "We'll go home soon. And **T**imely?" George asked. "That's is out." He answered his own question with a loud fart that sounded like a drum roll. Everyone laughed. "Hey! I'll howl my heart out back home in Pennsylvania."

Bailey beamed with pride. George had become such a good sport.

Aunt Jetta smiled. "We stepped over R. How about **R?** Is howling **R**elevant?" Aunt Jetta continued. "**R**elevant to the education of the stoats?"

"What if we transform it into general arts education?" Miles wondered.

"Howling could be part of a multi-disciplinary arts program like music, dance, drawing, painting and sculpting," Cosmo suggested.

"What about a choir program?" Bailey asked. "If they learn to harmonize with one another by singing maybe that will help them live in harmony."

"Like being on the same vibration?" Cosmo rolled his eyes.

"These are all great ideas. We should definitely explore an arts curriculum." Aunt Jetta loved the brainstorming. "Try to remember when you really had fun learning something." She encouraged the group. "Who taught you? And what? Anyone have a fond memory of learning?"

"The farmer taught me to tend our livestock," said Mitch, "with verbal commands and with a whistle. I learned the cue for 'walk up' when he wanted me to bring in the flock; the cue for 'look back', when a sheep was left behind; and the cue for 'circle the flock' to keep them cozied together. When I got it right, he gave me a treat." He looked at Aunt Jetta. "That made it easy."

Aunt Jetta nodded with vigor. "Yes," she said, "reward can be a powerful tool for teaching. It helps motivate learning."

"True. But you know what?" Mitch was not done. "The acrobatics? I taught myself. I tried agai-n and agai-n, until I got it right. Repeti-ition did it. But we've got the expert right here, among us. Right, Leo? What about you? You went through such transformation. You learned so much."

Leo smirked. "Right, mate. I used to be no different than the stoats. If I can learn, so can they." He looked at Mitch with gratitude. "Having a compassionate and confidence-building teacher made a huge impact. You, Mitch, taught me responsibility. I deplore my mistakes and live with the regret of killing kiwis, but now I try to do better... *You*, Mitch, took me in and made me boss of the food barn. Appreciate you, *mate*!"

Mitch gave him a high-five.

"As for learning the haka?" Leo grinned. "I just imitated the natives."

"Should we ask Sam what *he* feels his kids should learn, where he feels they could improve?" Mr. Guinness was proactive.

"Ask the stoats? Brilliant!" Aunt Jetta took his suggestion to heart. Anyone else?"

"What about you, Aunt Jetta?" Mr. Guinness asked. "What are your thoughts?"

"For starters," she said, "Let me show you *where* I envision the school."

She led a procession to the most perfect spot she could think of, right outside the fence where the stage had been on Friday night. The kowhai tree with its golden flowers attracted tuis, wood pigeons, and bellbirds—so there would be a lovely ambience. This location was easily accessible for the stoats and their teachers. And just like with the show, the school would not interfere with farming activities.

"Mitch," she asked, "is this okay with you? Will we be out of your way?"

Mitch nodded. He appreciated that Aunt Jetta considered his daily logistics. He had his work to do. The school would be hers.

"Leo, would you mind opening the gate for me every morning that school is in session?" Aunt Jetta asked.

"No problem, mate," Leo said. "I'll be happy to close it, too."

"Now to the program," Aunt Jetta paused and took a deep breath. She felt tightness in her stomach, so she took three more deep breaths to regroup. She believed that she had the strength to handle this task, that this was her fate, her karma, her destiny. She would rely on her instincts, her will to make a difference and her desire to help. "I need a moment to process all of your ideas and think this through. So, before I fill you in, shall we take a potty break?"

They all did and came back quickly, eager to hear more.

"I want to make school really fun," Aunt Jetta began.

"Fun?" George snickered. "No punishment? No disciplinary actions? No visits to the principal's shed?"

"Hear me out!" Aunt Jetta laughed, sure of herself. "All my life, I have observed my family. They were most content and lighthearted when they had dinner together, played games or waltzed to music so loud my ears hurt. It seems eating, playing, dancing and arts in general are essential for well-being. Why not apply this to our school curriculum? So we'll do food and play. The message of living in harmony will be the theme of all our activities. We'll reform the stoat appetites with patience, persistence and persuasion. They may be so busy with learning that they'll forget about food raiding sprees."

"How so?" Mr. Guinness raised his brow. "What do you mean, exactly?"

"Three things." Aunt Jetta sat with a very straight posture, gesturing with her right paw to underscore her words. "**First,** every morning, we offer food for the body. If we ask them not to eat kiwi and penguin eggs, we must present other choices. I'm thinking slugs, grubs, wire worms, cockroaches and rats." She had the menu planned. "Katydids, crickets, and grasshoppers. Snails are treats for stoats. And there are plenty of them. None of them are in danger of extinction. In fact, there are too many. Some are garden pests."

"Would you want my leftovers?" Leo asked. "They'll have an extra bony crunch."

"Great!" Aunt Jetta said, but cautioned him, "The pieces need to be small,"

"No problem," Leo said, showing off his incisors and his claws. "I'll rip them into bite size portions."

"Thank you, Leo!" Aunt Jetta was relieved her ideas had support. She needed community backing. Big time.

"I wonder though," Aunt Jetta said, "if we have a big turnout, will there be enough food for *before and after* school? Appetites could be immense." She tried to remain calm. "My school is about controlling appetites." Her mind revved. "Angus, could you pitch in too?"

"No worries, mate." Angus stretched out his hooves. "We've got it covered. She'll be right!" He pointed to two large buckets with closed lids and grinned. "We'll have those filled by tomorrow." Aunt Jetta dropped her shoulders and relaxed.

Cockroach—*Periplaneta americana*

"Your **S.** turns to snacking and the **M.** into munching," George giggled and rolled over on his side.

"No one can focus when they're hungry," Aunt Jetta said.

"When you have treats," Lexi whispered, "you have their attention."

"The way to someone's heart is through the stomach," Bailey added approvingly. "That's a Pennsylvania Dutch expression."

Aunt Jetta got a quick drink of water. Her mouth was dry from all that talking.

"**Second,**" she continued to address her audience, "We'll play games and dance. I'm thinking hop-scotch, poi ball, and relay races with four stoats per team. They'll learn sportsmanship and cooperation. Games will teach them to take turns, to play fair and to get along. We shake paws after each game, even when one side gets whooped. And if kiwis and penguins are visiting—I'm thinking down the line here—we will have mixed species races."

"So the **R.** turns into running, right?" George mused.

"And the **S.** into sports." Rosie hopped up and down.

"There should be rewards or prizes." Aunt Jetta was not done yet, "but I have not thought that through."

"You mentioned dancing? What kind?" Leo asked. "Should we teach the haka to the stoats?"

Aunt Jetta smiled. "Why not? It's their nature to dance alone and in pairs. Stoats stand on their hind legs and gambol with berserk and cajoling steps. Dancing will bring us all together."

"It certainly brought us together," Miles said to Cosmo and winked at Leo.

"Here is my **third point,**" Aunt Jetta continued, "We offer food for the mind. Stoats are like all of us. They love stimulation. They, too, want to go on journeys of discovery. We will explore new ideas and sing together."

George started laughing. "The **T.** turned into Tricking; tricking them into learning with food and games."

"I call it teaching with clever methods," Aunt Jetta said.

Mr. Guinness, Mitch and Leo did not have one word of critique. In unison they said, "Go for it, Aunt Jetta!"

But George admonished her, "You are a softie. This doesn't sound like school. This sounds like fun!"

"Why can't school be fun?" Aunt Jetta asked. "Isn't it better that way?"

George insisted, "What if those stoats are unruly? What if someone gets out of line? You should carry a paddle. We may have to pull their ears and tails to make them understand."

"On the contrary, George! This school will be without punishment," Aunt Jetta said. "No shaming. No time outs. The letter **M.** in SMART, if I may reframe it, George—**M.** stands for **M**otivation. I hope we can motivate the students."

"Wait a minute," Cosmo called out. He sat down, raised his paw and looked up in the sky. For a minute. A really long minute.

"Yes?" Aunt Jetta probed.

"This is far out, guys. Really far out." Cosmo grinned. "This just might become an academy of happiness. What do you know?"

Miles clapped. Leo undulated his tail with pleasure. Mitch embraced Aunt Jetta. Mr. Guinness threw her a kiss. Bailey smiled. Lexi and Rosie hugged each other. George howled his approval.

Aunt Jetta was jubilant. She loved to be useful in life. She was going to be the head mistress in a school that the stoats would flock to every day. Her goal was to develop a relationship with each and every stoat kid. And if these kids learned to avoid the kiwi and penguin eggs, maybe they would inspire their elders with new ideas. And *that*, Aunt Jetta thought, would be terrific. On weekends, she could help Mitch herd sheep. New Zealand was truly her heaven. She smiled.

"May we excuse ourselves?" Miles bowed. "We have a project that needs our attention."

Cosmo picked up his satchel with the art supplies. Whiskers forward, the two cats strutted to the food barn. They had an agenda of their own. They wanted to make something grand to commemorate their visit from America. A monument of stones maybe, stacked up like a pyramid? Stones were symbols of permanence. Maybe something with color? For sure, something totally new. The cats closed the barn door behind them.

*****

In the shearing shed, dinner was delicious. Afterwards, the dogs settled down for the night—Mitch with his boys and Aunt Jetta, with Mr. Guinness, Lexi and Rosie, Bailey and George. Just as George dozed off, he whispered in Bailey's ear. She, in turn, got Aunt Jetta's attention and whispered to her.

"That's a great idea." Aunt Jetta smiled. "We'll do it tomorrow."

"Do what?" Lexi asked.

"It's a surprise." Aunt Jetta closed her eyes.

⊙⊙ Chapter 18: The First Day ⊙⊙

Both early risers, Mitch and Aunt Jetta had breakfast together: leftover shepherd's pie with chicken gravy. They stepped outside and watched the sun illuminate the sky in pink. Mitch gathered his sheep for their walk to the meadows in the hills. Aunt Jetta stood at the door and waved. She looked forward to her new life. She had only been in New Zealand less than a day, but already it felt like home.

A cacophony of ecstatic squawks and a wave of pungent, fresh sea aroma announced the day's first arrivals. Aunt Jetta turned her head to take in a most unusual sight. Twelve rockhopper penguins stood at the gate, crooning. They were on time—early, actually.

"Aunt Jetta!" they called. "We are here to meet someone by the name of Aunt Jetta. We've come to work with her."

Two feet tall, the rockhoppers had big heads, blood-red eyes, orange beaks, short thick necks and stream-lined bodies. When they shook their heads, their yellow tasseled brows flew up into a halo encircling their mohawks of yellow and black spiked feathers. They looked like rock stars. However, these creatures were not out of control or crazy. They stood close together patiently preening, waiting to be let in.

Rockhopper Portrait #1
—*Eudyptes crestatus*

Rockhopper Portrait #2

Rockhopper Portrait #3

Rockhopper Portrait #4

"Welcome! I'm Aunt Jetta." She opened the gate—Leo had shown her how. Seeing so many of them thrilled her. How did these rockhoppers have the foresight to come in such numbers? "Pleased to meet you and ever so delighted you are here. Come this way, please. May I offer you some water?"

The rockhoppers entered the compound, not waddling like the blue penguins, but bouncing high on their pink feet with massive energy. Three of them, a bit taller than the others, separated from the group and checked out the three barns and the shed, then looped back around through the gate to inspect the hot spring by the rocks. It was a survey of sorts. The other nine rallied around the water buckets and took turns drinking.

The cousins, startled by the noise, came outside with Mr. Guinness in the lead. They all sat down and stared.

"What colorful creatures!" Lexi exclaimed in wonder.

"I bet they are really smart." Rosie admired smart people.

"I imagine they do S.M.A.R.T. as well." Mr. Guinness winked.

"Smart stoats may admire their rockhopper teachers," Lexi beamed.

And Bailey added, "I do hope the stoats adore them and that they aren't too much for the rockhoppers' taste."

"We'll find out soon enough." George grinned.

Aunt Jetta waved 'good morning' to her family, but had no time to talk. After all twelve rockhoppers had their fill of water, she led them into the shearing shed stage room and closed the door. This was her meet-and-greet with the new teachers, her getting-to-know-you and the first in-service session for the school agenda.

Outside, the cousins wondered while they were waiting.

"What they are doing in there?" asked George.

"She'll outline the program," Mr. Guinness said, "and instruct them on what she wants."

"What is taking them so long?" Rosie paced back and forth, restlessly.

"Do I hear singing?" Lexi turned her head to hear better.

After a while, the door opened. Aunt Jetta paraded out first. The penguins hopped behind her in a straight line, cheering loudly. "Yesses!" and "We shall do this!" and "Save our species and the kiwis too!" There was energy and enthusiasm in their leaps.

"How did it go?" Mr. Guinness asked, though he thought he knew the answer.

"Terrific!" Aunt Jetta was jubilant. "We can do this together. The rockhoppers know about life on land *and* in the sea, about the balance of dangers and opportunities. That gives them an incredible perspective on life's possibilities."

As if to emphasize Aunt Jetta's enthusiasm, the bird sentinels sounded a signal, louder than yesterday. Everyone turned to the totara grove and the rustling in the underbrush. Aunt Jetta had hoped for this. Here they came—four stoat mothers, arm-in-arm, with a rambunctious gaggle of kids behind them—a squeaking avalanche of fur rolling through the gate in a cloud of musty aroma. Rosie tried to count how many there were, but gave up. The shoving, squealing and giggling mob made her head spin. The stoat kids were adorable: brown pelt, white bellies, short tails, round ears, sweet faces—so very cute.

The moment the mothers saw the rockhoppers, they rose on their hind legs and froze. Their kids tumbled over each other and landed on their tiny butts and bellies and stared in shock and awe. These penguins exuded authority. They demanded attention. And they got it.

"Mamas and kids!" the rockhoppers vocalized. "Welcome to our first day of school!" They shook their golden eyebrow feathers vigorously. Loud calls and ecstatic movements followed. The penguins quivered. They bowed. They pointed

First School Day

their heads skyward. They extended their flippers and made a series of loud calls, their bills wide open whilst swinging their heads from side to side, transfixing the stoats with their display.

"What a performance!" Mr. Guinness whispered in Bailey's ear. "Well orchestrated, I say."

"Yes! They are in such unison," Bailey whispered back. "I wasn't sure if I could tell them apart at first, but look! I can see they are all different. That one has a spot on his neck. That one's beak is a deeper orange."

"Ah, yes," Mr. Guinness enjoyed finding the distinctions. "One has a scar on the left foot. And that one has it on the right."

"Oh Guinny, isn't this beyond belief?" Bailey turned to him, her eyes brimming with joy.

School activities were about to begin. It was critical the stoats did not get bored, especially not on the first day. Aunt Jetta gestured for the rockhopper ensemble to line up, six on her left side and six on her right side. "Listen up!" She addressed the lounging stoats. "We are going to start things off with some music. Please, sing along! The more, the merrier! Let's get loud!"

Flanked by the twelve, Aunt Jetta started singing. The rockhoppers joined in, twirling their tassels.

"It doesn't matter if you are from the wilderness
Or from the mountains
Underground, of the sea
Or the town
Sing along with me

And if you are from the tops of trees
Or the sands of the desert
Of the night
Of the day
Come and play
Join the band with me

We get together in all weather
And we play and sing this song
Lalalalalalalalala
We're striving to be better
With an open heart together
So we sing
Lalalalalalalalala.

It doesn't matter where you're from
There is nobody like you
We all swoon to the same silver moon

Come on dance with me

When I open up my heart
Then I will find you
No more us
No more them
We begin
Come on sing with me

We get together in all weather
And we play and sing this song
Lalalalalalalalala
And we're striving to be better
With an open heart together
So we sing
Lalalalalalalalala

Even though the night is dark
The sun will be rising
And that sun's
Shining on everyone
Come on sing with me

When you open up your heart
Then I will find you
No more us
No more them
We begin
Come on sing with me

We get together in all weather
And we play and sing this song
Lalalalalalalalala
And we're striving to be better
With an open heart together

So we sing
Lalalalalalalalala."

The stoat mothers had never ever heard anything so cheerful, so uplifting and so inclusive. Right here, they decided that this song was for *them,* to sing in the underbrush. The 'Lalala-ing' was easy. They squeaked along, arms linked, swaying from side to side. Maybe later, they could learn all the other words. Happy day!

"Excellent!"

"Bravo!"

"Well done!"

Aunt Jetta allowed herself to bask in the applause, but just for a moment. It was time to get the school day going. As the applause quieted, she raised her front paws and shouted. "Do you know why we are all here today?"

There was mumbling within the stoat assembly.

"Mama told us to come."

"Daddy did, too."

"My brothers all came."

"All my sisters, too."

"No clue."

"We are here today," Aunt Jetta proclaimed with a glowing smile, "to play games and do art projects!"

A cheer rang out.

"We are here to learn new things. We are here to live together better, happier and with more fun than ever. We are here to learn more about each other and our neighbors, especially the kiwis and penguins. They need our help."

"Why?" asked a stoat kid in the front.

"The kiwis and penguins are our neighbors. But not enough of them are surviving. They may soon be all dead. And that is bad for New Zealand and the world."

"The world? Where is that?"

"It's right here, where we all live. And this school is where we learn to help our neighbors, help them survive and thrive." Aunt Jetta smiled.

"We can be heroes," another stoat kid said.

"Sounds glamorous!" a third one said.

"In our school, there will be fun with different foods and activities. This is your reward for doing the one thing we ask of you: help us keep the kiwis and penguins alive! Can I count on you? I hope you will promise."

There was mumbling in the stoat crowd.

Aunt Jetta did not expect instant success, but she hoped that her message would sink in. She believed in the power of a promise.

"Won't we go hungry? What else is there?"

"In life, my dear students, there are always options," Aunt Jetta said. She signaled to the cousins to hand out the mouse meat snacks. The stoats dug in. They munched and chewed and burped. Never had they tasted such a delicacy! The rockhoppers stood watch keeping an eye on their school breakfast crowd.

Rosie circled the stoats as they were snacking. She wanted to do the M. part of SMART. Measuring. How many students showed up on the first day? She counted 64 stoats, including the mothers: fifteen kids per mom. That was a lot of stoats.

"Today we shall start to get to know one another. Let's play games and have some fun!" Aunt Jetta announced. "We have special guests who came all the way from across the ocean to be with us." She introduced the cousins. "They have prepared activities just for you." She pointed to the various set-ups on the meadow. "Go and enjoy!"

The stoat mothers and their kids got up to check out the options. And there were so many options!

Mr. Guinness had set up start and finish lines for relay races, instructing the stoat kids to pass small sticks by mouth from runner to runner. It almost seemed like kissing. Mr. Guinness had wanted the event to be structured in teams of four, but that worked only at the beginning. The stoats could not wait their turn. They all picked up sticks and ran around with them, throwing them in the air and catching them. He decided to let them do their thing: it was the first day after all.

George gave piggyback rides while Bailey organized the queue. George had wanted their ride to be a surprise, but he had howled about it in his sleep to the wonderment of Mitch in particular. He carried the stoat babes around in a large circle.

They loved that. They were holding on to his fur for dear life. There were lots of giggles when one toppled off. When his hip started hurting from all the running—that old hunting injury—he laid down and let the stoat pups clamber all over him.

Miles and Cosmo had made a sign on a stick. It read "*Couleurs Ici,*" and in small letters underneath, "Paint Station." They were not sure if this was a proper translation, but it was good enough!

On a bench they laid out two paint cans and two brushes. Both cans were full of white fence paint, though one was tinted pink using crushed winterberries. Burlap canvases were spread out on the grass. For self-portraits, maybe? But the stoat kids were more interested in body painting—ears or tails, or both. The cats were inspired by the kids' exuberance. The stoats wanted their backs, bellies and butts done in stripes or dots. Some washed off the paint in the hot spring, and came right back for more. Miles and Cosmo were kept very busy.

The rockhoppers offered hopping lessons, of course. High hops, long hops, side hops, backward hops, somersaults, cartwheels and belly flop hops. For the youngest stoats, the rockhoppers made a grid with sticks for a cute little stoat-sized hopscotch.

The pigs joined in the fun, too. They left their barn doors wide open. Everyone could hear Mozart's "Eine kleine Nachtmusik" blasting from the rafters. The pigs danced around the stoats in a circle, hopping on two feet, holding paws and squealing with joy.

What an extraordinary event this had become!

With the squeaking and giggling and cajoling sounds traveling up the hillside, Mitch and his helpers brought the herd home early so they would not miss out. The first day of school had become a fine carnival. Aunt Jetta was pleased.

Without any warning, Sam the Great, came swaggering into the compound. When he saw the rockhoppers towering over his family, he stopped in his tracks, mesmerized. Lexi ran to greet him, to ease any apprehensions, and to show him around the activities. When they came to the paint station, Sam locked eyes with Miles. With a grand gesture, Miles handed Sam his paintbrush. This was new for Sam. He applied pink paint liberally all over his belly. Then Cosmo traded him the other brush. Sam painted his hind feet white. When he was done, he stood erect and, with a toothy grin, presented himself to his family: Sam the Magnificent.

As he twirled around, he noticed shadows overhead. A gliding swoosh of air ruffled his fur. A pair of white-chested albatrosses with enormous wingspans soared in from the sea, and descended gently onto the meadow.

Albatrosses Posing—*Diomedeidae*

Sam whistled alarm to his family and ran for cover under the nearest bush. His family was so busy having fun, no one noticed. Seeing his panic, one rockhopper bounced over to his hiding spot and bent down low. "You're alright, mate. Do not be afraid. Those are albatrosses. They are here to dance."

Sam looked at him, unsure, and rolled his eyes before he rejoined his family, who did not have a care in the world.

And without delay or introduction, the albatrosses began *their* show, an elegant display of grandeur: clapping, clicking and rubbing beaks; nodding and dipping heads; stretching wings; bob-rutting around each other; preening-under-the-wing, right, then left and again; whipping up and down on their webbed feet; displaying their gape; performing a sky-point and culminating their display in loud clattering sky-call. It was a wondrous dance of joy!

Albatrosses Dancing

The stoats screeched with enthusiasm. The pigs squealed with merriment. The sheep baa-ed with pleasure. The cousins applauded with all their might. Mitch and Leo could not believe their eyes—their farm was the center of a theatrical production! This school was *"choice bro."*

Albatrosses Kissing

As a finale, the albatrosses extended their wings as an enormous backdrop for the school staff of twelve rockhoppers and Aunt Jetta in the middle.

"This ends our first day," Aunt Jetta announced. "Let's sing together once more." Repetition, as in all learning, was a good thing.

With her rockhopper Rock Star Ensemble she sang the Stoat School Song again. Some of the more musically inclined stoats picked up the refrain and blared it into the sky. "Lalalala!"

Sam whistled for his clan to head out back toward the totara grove.

"See you tomorrow!" Aunt Jetta shouted after them. "Take a snack for the way home!"

Angus and Aliya waited on either side of the gate, each with a bucket, the lids half-capped, filled with a crawly jumble of cockroaches, slugs, grubs, wire worms and dead lizards. Yesterday evening, Angus and Aliya had planned this with Aunt Jetta. They had asked their flock to collect the goodies while grazing and to deposit them into an empty trough. While hoofing out the treats, Angus shouted, "Let's be good neighbors to the kiwis and penguins!" He winked at Aliya. She smiled back at him. They both loved that their sheep were involved in this campaign.

After the stoats had cleared out, the place was a mess—the relay sticks, the knocked-over paint pots, and the hopscotch pebbles. Thankfully, all the paint had been brushed onto the stoats, so there were no major spills. With enthusiasm, the rockhoppers tidied up. In no time, the place looked spotless and green. During a second quick in-service to reflect on their first day, the rockhoppers decided that tomorrow, before going home, they would teach the stoats a "clean-up" game. Their reward would be an extra snack.

Aunt Jetta took a moment to sit down. She felt exhausted, but at the same time totally exhilarated. She was so glad to have dared to come on this adventure. Her heart sang. What a worthwhile cause! Thank you to Condor Chiara! Chiara Mia! Hallelujah!

Mitch joined her. "So… will you do this every day?" he asked.

"In various forms and with the rockhoppers' help, yes," Aunt Jetta smiled. "Why not?"

Mitch put his arm around her. "You may just change our world."

Chapter 19: Giving

With the stoats gone, the rockhoppers on their way back to the sea, the pigs safe in their barn and the sheep baa-ing softly, Miles and Cosmo took Mr. Guinness to the side.

Miles reminded him, "Condor Chiara is planning to take us back tonight," Miles said.

"Yes." Mr. Guinness sighed. "Saying goodbye makes my heart heavy."

"*Moi aussi.* Me too. But let's lighten things up." The cats had mischievous looks on their faces. "We have planned a magnificent farewell ceremony to honor our hosts."

"What do you have in mind?" Mr. Guinness asked. He loved their gallant vibe.

"May we suggest a thank-you address, followed by a presentation of mementos that Cosmo and I have made?" Miles's eyes glowed.

"You two never cease to amaze me."

Cosmo smiled. "Would you like to see them?"

"Of course." Life was so much more fun with these cats around.

Miles and Cosmo took Mr. Guinness into the food barn—his first time in there. It smelled of hay.

Cosmo spoke with excitement. "A deadline always gets us going. *N'est-ce-pas,* Miles? Urgency makes the ideas flow," he declared, his chest swelling with pride. "We made these last night." He took a very deep breath.

"May we present the school banner?" Miles extended his right paw.

On the far wall, hanging on a cord made of braided wool, was a drawing. It was done in blue pencil on a canvas of feed sack paper. Bold strokes with robust shading outlined three silhouettes: a stoat in the middle, erect, one foot forward, between a kiwi and a penguin. The kiwi touched the stoat's paw with her beak, the penguin touched the stoat's other paw with her flipper. It was a scene of joy, friendship and congeniality, depicting the eternal dance of life.

"I love it." Mr. Guinness was in awe.

Reconciliation School Banner

"We made sure it is sturdy. It's reinforced with wool crocheting and backed with burlap." The cats grinned. "It can be rolled up to be stored overnight. When school is in session, Aunt Jetta can hang it outside from the totara tree. We call the piece, 'Untitled.'"

"This is so *apropos!*" Mr. Guinness's voice was deep and full of praise. "But why 'Untitled'?"

"We figured," Miles spoke first, "The stoat kids and their teachers can have a naming contest—with Aunt Jetta's approval, of course."

"The act of naming is powerful. It will give them a sense of pride." Cosmo added, "And we made presents for our spectacular hosts."

Cosmo pointed to the table in the center of the food barn. Five oversized collars were laid out flat. Cosmo had incorporated nature's bounty into his artwork. He had strung last season's red winterberries onto thinly braided threads of wool of all colors interspersed with beads from his satchel. For cameos, he used polished macadamia nuts. The collars were large enough to slip over the head to hang low like necklaces.

"We made one for Aunt Jetta, Mitch, Leo, Angus, and Aliya. Maybe they'll wear them on Friday nights to remember us."

Mr. Guinness ran outside and called in his troupe to admire the pieces.

Miles and Cosmo proclaimed in unison, "We would like you, dogs, to present the collars to our hosts."

"Thank you." Mr. Guinness accepted that honor for his cousins. "With great pleasure."

Carefully, the dogs carried the collars outside. In preparation for the ceremony, Mr. Guinness called on Aunt Jetta and the New Zealanders. "Please, do join us for a moment!"

He waited for everyone to be seated, all in a row in the New Zealand grass.

"Dear friends," Mr. Guinness began. "We thank you from the bottom of our hearts for taking us in and for letting us be part of your lives and for becoming part of ours. We hope we have made a difference in a good way. As a memento of our visit, we would like for you to have these collars, paw-made by Miles and Cosmo." He bowed to Aunt Jetta and decorated her neck.

Lexi offered a collar to Leo with a kiss. "Thank you, Lexi." Leo teared up. To hide his emotion, being a tom-cat after all, he turned to Miles and Cosmo. "In Maori, gift is 'koha.'"

Rosie gave a collar to Aliya. Because the ewe was so tall, Rosie needed a running hop to reach.

Her tail wagging, Bailey gave one to Angus with a warm smile.

George pawed one over Mitch's white fur mane with a yodel.

"Dear guests and frie-ends." Mitch stood up to address the group. He looked grand with the decoration around his neck. "Your pre-sence at our farm has been a life-changing event." He drew out his vowels extra-long. "Leo and I…" he put his arm around the barn cat, "and all the sheep and pigs on this farm, we've had the time of our lives. We appreciate your noble inten-tions. And thank you for bringing Aunt Jetta to live here. She is a gift to all of us." Mitch bowed to her. Aunt Jetta smiled. "We wish you we-ell on your trip home. And we do hope our paths will cross again, my frie-ends."

The sound of huge wings churning the air caused them all to look skyward. Condor Chiara was arriving with her squadron. As they landed, the triangular white patches under their wings glowed in the setting sun. The condors lined up for the cousins to hop on. Angus and Aliya baaed farewell. The pigs came running out of their barn, twirling their tails and oinking goodbye. Leo waved and grinned. Mitch and his helpers barked. Aunt Jetta blew kisses.

"One last thing," Lexi shouted, "now I know what the 'new' in New Zealand means. It means new for new beginnings, new possibilities and a whole new world!"

"Are you sure?" Rosie had her doubts. "We'll have to verify that when we get home."

"Ah!" Lexi exhaled. "When we get home."

The cousins settled into their feather baskets, readying themselves for departure. The tui birds began singing about the sun on the mountain tops, the wind in the trees and the joy in their hearts. The snipes vibrated their tail feathers, drumming out a throbbing, rattling sound like a galloping horse. Bellbirds, olive green with a dark purplish sheen on their heads, with black wings and tails, chimed in three tones, just like ringing bells.

The condors lifted off, veering eastward into the evening sky.

Goodbye, New Zealand.

Chapter 20: Apologies

Back home in California, the autumn sun was setting. The Septet lounged around the chimenea on the patio—Rosie and Lexi flat on their bellies, George on his back with all four paws in the air, Mr. Guinness and Bailey on their sides. The cats were curled up next to each other. The air was crisp and not too chilly, but the scent of flowers was no longer. In the distant hills, the sugar maples blazoned forth in a spectacular show of orange, red and gold. Fall had come.

"We accomplished our mission," said Mr. Guinness. "I expect the school will continue to succeed."

Bailey raised her head and looked at the evening sky. "Condor Chiara will tell the hummingbirds about Aunt Jetta and her school. I wonder what they'll think."

"I wonder if the stoats include rats in their diet now." George stretched so that his nails stuck out.

"Leo counts the kiwis around the farm," Rosie said.

"And the rockhoppers are checking on the little blue penguins." Lexi jingled her collar. "I'm so grateful you all came to visit. This was an awesome Thanksgiving that we did not have."

Miles and Cosmo had their eyes closed, but were not asleep. Even though these cats could be outspoken in public, privately they often felt insecure. Both questioned themselves about their talents, what they did with it and if they realized it to their full potential. Doubt about the quality of their work tormented them at times. They worried about their sluggishness when they did not start projects first thing in the morning. They tortured themselves for laziness after roaming the neighborhood instead of working, for idling time away by grooming each other, or—worst case scenario—by sleeping all day. Inactivity filled with procrastination could masquerade as soul-searching. Will our art please anyone? Does it do any good? But the events in New Zealand had lifted their spirits. Reminiscing about them made the cats purr intensely. They basked in the afterglow of the joy their art had generated— the school banner and the celebration collars. It reminded them that art has meaning and is transformative.

As it was the last night of this visit, Mr. Guinness wanted to make it a special evening. "Let's have a party," he said. "A 'Jokes and Riddles' party."

"What a great idea, Guinny!" Lexi gushed. "No need for TV ever again!"

Rosie threw Lexi a doubtful look, but kept quiet.

"*Jouer avec des mots*? Play with words?" Miles and Cosmo opened their eyes and grinned. "*Merveilleux!*"

"Jokes? Yes! Riddles? Nooh!" George turned over and grumbled. "I'm too tired to strain my brain."

"Come on, George! Be a good sport!" Bailey nudged him in the side and turned to Mr. Guinnness. "What's your riddle, Guinny?"

Mr. Guinness raised his head. "Okay," he said. "I have an end, but no beginning. I have a home, but no family." He paused. "I have space, but no room. I never speak, but I can make any word, in any language. What am I?"

George blurted out. "That makes no sense!"

"No family? No room?" Lexi choked up. "So sad!"

Rosie jumped up and down. "That's a tough one, Guinny! I should know the answer."

Mr. Guinness held his chin. He enjoyed puzzling his crowd.

The cats scrunched their noses. "No idea."

Bailey looked at Mr. Guinness with admiring eyes. He was the most intelligent dog she had ever met. "Is this, maybe, related to your Silicon Valley work?"

Mr. Guinness nodded.

The cats smirked. "Tell us!"

"It's a keyboard," Mr. Guinness smiled with glee.

"What?" Lexi was clueless.

"Oh!" Rosie cheered. "A keyboard like on a computer!" "You are talking about the 'end' key and the 'home' key and the space bar. Of course!"

Mr. Guinness grinned. It was so good to be home.

Bailey wanted to make the most of her last night. She spoke up. "Can I be next?" She loved the exchanging of ideas and looking at things in a new way. Back home in Pennsylvania, George was her buddy, but not really her thinking partner. He did not get her thinking like Mr. Guinness did.

But George admired Bailey to no end. "You know riddles?" He was amazed.

"I do," she smiled. "What animal has more lives than a cat?"

"Is that possible?" The cats groaned.

"A frog," Bailey said.

"A frog? *Pourquoi*?" Miles asked.

"Because he keeps on croaking."

Pacific Tree Frog—
Pseudacris regilla

"Croaking?" George belly-laughed. "That's really good, Bailey."

"Your turn, George," Bailey passed the baton.

George cradled his head in his paws. After a long minute he belched one up. "Okay," he said. "What's a cat's favorite color?" He winked at Miles and Cosmo.

These cats treasured their secrets. What did George, the dog, know about their private preferences, predilections and inclinations? Mr. Guinness, Bailey, Rosie and Lexi raised their brows and shrugged. George let them all stew on it for one delightful moment. Then he blasted out. "It's purr-ple! Get it?" He laughed so hard about his own joke that snot dripped from his nose.

Everyone applauded. George bowed, of course.

"Can I have a turn?" Lexi was eager to go next. "This one is also for you two, Miles and Cosmo." Lexi paraded in front of the cats, her collar jingling as she moved. "Do you know when a dog goes 'moo'?"

Heads shaking all around.

Lexi wiggled her mane in flirty triumph. "Dogs go 'moo,' when they learn another language."

"Magnifique!" The cats were amused.

"What?" George needed an explanation.

"You know, cows speak the 'moo' language. So when dogs learn to speak 'moo,' that's when they moo. Get it?"

George groaned and collapsed on the patio.

Lexi loved this party and did not want it to end. "Someone else! Cosmo! Miles!"

"I have one." Cosmo said, taking the lead for the cats. "What falls and does not break? And what breaks and does not fall?"

Miles gave his buddy a knowing look. "Rain falls and does not break."

Cosmo smiled at him. "You get my drift."

"But the second part? I don't know."

"You're on the right track." Cosmo winked.

"Does it have to do with the cosmos?" Miles asked. "You're always on a higher plane, *mon ami*."

Tail straight up with the tip slightly bent, Cosmo nodded. "Night falls, but does not break and day breaks, but does not fall."

"Très bien." Miles rose to his feet, clapping. He cleared his throat. "Here is my riddle. Without wings I fly. Without eyes I see. Without legs I climb. I can be more frightening than any beast, stronger than any foe. I'm cunning and tall. I can bring tremendous joy. And, in the end, I rule it all. Who am I?"

"Scary," Lexi said.

"I don't get it." George made a face. "I just don't get it."

Bailey whispered, "I don't either. Maybe it's cat humor."

The dogs were at their wits' end.

But Cosmo held up one paw. "Ohhh! I've got this one!" He stared at the sky. "Or maybe I don't. Umm. Wait! It's a stretch! But seriously! It's about having ideas, isn't it? The 'I' stands for idea or imagination. Dreaming up something. All kinds of things."

"Like we dreamed up our show?" Lexi enthused with her eyes.

"And Condor Chiara envisioned the founding of the school," Bailey added.

"It's also about art projects. Imagination is the key. Maybe even for how we conduct our lives?" Cosmo hi-fived Miles. "Fabulous!"

"Rosie! Your turn." Mr. Guinness put his paw around her. She shook it off and took a step away from him.

"Rosie?!" Mr. Guinness frowned. "What's wrong?"

Rosie started pacing. "I need to get this off my chest. I can't stand it anymore." She panted.

What could be the matter? "Calm down, Rosie," urged Mr. Guinness.

Rosie stopped in her tracks. "I can't," she said.

They all raised their heads. Rosie hung hers and stared at the mulch on the patio. She dropped onto her butt, sat and bit her toe nails. "In front of all of you... I must do this."

"Do what?"

"I need to apologize to Lexi." Rosie had everyone's attention. Her lips quivered.

"To me?" Lexi sat down in front of Rosie. "For what?"

Rosie pressed her lips together. "I did you wrong, Lexi," she said after a moment of stiff silence. Her voice cracked. "For a long time, I've thought of you as a TV bum, a couch potato and a lightweight. I didn't take you seriously."

Lexi's eyes grew to the size of water bowls. "Oh?"

Rosie bowed her head and looked at her belly. "I was wrong. Dead wrong." She wiped her eyes with her paw and hid her face.

"Rosie!" Lexi nudged her with her nose to gaze into Rosie's eyes. "You are my best friend."

Rosie cleared her throat and looked at Lexi. "You, Lexi, are brave. You stuck your neck out. In the middle of the night, you walked into that stoat camp. You acted on what you felt in your heart, what you were passionate about—making life better for the kiwis. I was wrong about you. I'm so sorry." Rosie began sobbing. Her shoulders shook.

"Wow!" George belched. "I didn't see *that* coming."

"*That* takes gumption," Bailey exhaled.

"My dear Rosie," Lexi said softly, "All these years, I knew what you thought of me. You made it clear, but I ignored it. You are smart, and well-read, but you can be very judgmental. We all can improve in many ways. Like, I got stronger in New Zealand. Don't be so hard on yourself now. I love you."

Rosie stopped sobbing. "Do you forgive me?"

"Of course, I do." Lexi gave her a kiss on the cheek.

Bailey and Mr. Guinness, sitting so close that they touched sides, smiled. Cosmo raised his paw for hi-fives all around. Miles groomed his whiskers, rubbed his chin, and then turned around to look at his tail. So much insight was remarkable.

"You guys," George said. "Enough of this lovey-dovey thing!" He farted, loud, long and pungent.

Mr. Guinness stood up. "All right," he said. "Everyone okay now?"

"No. Not okay." Lexi bit her lip. Her eyes narrowed to a slit. She turned her back to the group. She kneeled down and buried her face in her paws.

"What is it with you now, Lexi? Ladies!!!" Mr. Guinness was concerned. "What's going on with you two?"

Lexi turned around and scratched her side. "You know what? I did what Rosie did. I judged the stoats. I hated them for their actions." Lexi paused. "But once I met them, I saw how they were creatures just like us. So I changed my mind about them. Now I feel really sad, because I should have apologized to them and I didn't." Her little voice broke. She hiccupped.

Wide-eyed, speechless and still, the family looked at Lexi.

"I'm so sorry about that. But there is nothing I can do about it now." Lexi cleared her throat. "The good thing is that we became friends and I have learned my lesson." She stared at her belly.

Bailey got up, scooted next to Lexi and rubbed her back. "This is not just about you or Rosie," she said. "When I first saw those penguins," she paused and chuckled, "I thought they were ridiculous. And what fine and noble creatures they turned out to be. We all could be thinking more kindly of others. And not just thinking kind thoughts. We should be doing acts of kindness."

Mr. Guinness smiled.

"Travel expands the mind. It definitely broadened my horizon. The world is fascinating in its diversity and we are all connected. I've learned so much about respecting others," Bailey said.

George scooted toward Bailey. "Respect everyone?!" He was all for being on good terms with his family, the kiwis, the penguins and even the stoats. "But what about the squirrels back home?" George harrumphed. "Need to talk that one over when we get back."

Bailey smiled wistfully.

"Rosie!" Mr. Guinness nudged her with his nose. "It's your turn now, my dear! Challenge us with a riddle!" He hoped showing off her knowledge would make her feel better.

"Okay," she said. She took a slow spin around the group. "I read this one in a book. It's from Greece and I love it, because it is so old and so true."

Mr. Guinness stretched his front legs in expectation. Bailey sat up straight. The cats paid attention.

"What walks on four legs in the morning, on two in the afternoon, and on three in the evening?"

"Is it us?" Lexi asked. "We walk on four legs most of the time. When we beg for treats we stand on two. We limp on three when we've stepped on something, and you guys," Lexi winked at George and Mr. Guinness, "You stand on three to pee. Am I right? Did I get it?" She giggled.

"No," Rosie said. "It's about humans. When they are little, they crawl on all fours. When they grow up, they walk on two legs. And when they get old, they will use a cane, a third leg."

Lexi who had been holding her breath in anticipation, exhaled. "Oh! I get it. I love our humans. I hope they never get old."

Miles raised his paw. "*Mes amis!*" he said. "One more!" He got up and walked around in a circle, looking everyone in the eye. "Why..." he paused. "Why are cats such good singers?"

"Hey," George mused. "Cats are not the only ones who can sing!"

"Let me take a guess," Bailey said. "Could it be," she looked Miles and Cosmo in the eye, "Because... they are so mew-sical?"

*****

Night fell. The temperature dropped. The cousins looked up and saw the splendor of the Milky Way—a wide belt of diamonds arched over the earth.

The Milky Way

Lexi mumbled, "Will the hummingbirds come back?"

Rosie reassured her, "They will. They do every spring,"

"We want to tell them what happened in New Zealand." Bailey stretched out next to George.

"I loved the trip." George nudged her in the neck.

"Maybe the hummingbirds will teach us another song," Miles mused.

"Do you think we could visit them in their winter place? Maybe we could even fly to the Galapagos Islands, see the blue-footed boobies and find out if their feet are really blue." Going there was Cosmo's dream.

"Same blue as the little penguins?" Lexi murmured.

"Perhaps Condor Chiara will arrange for another trip." Mr. Guinness stood up. "Let us go inside and get some sleep." He invited his troupe to follow him. "Shall we dream of what new adventures are to come? The choice is ours."

Glossary of Foreign Words

French

Absolument [ab-so-leu-mang]—absolutely
À-propos [ahh-proh-poh]—relevant, appropriate
À la George [aah-laa George]—in the way George would do it
Alors! [ah-lor]—okay! Listen up!
Anticonstitutionnellement [anti-con-sti-too-sh-on-nell-mon]—unconstitutionally
Artiste [aar-teest-eh]—artist
Bêtise [bai-tee-zah]—nonsense
Bien sûr [bee-en sur]—of course
Bonjour mes amis [bown zhoor mayz ah-me]—hello my friends
Certainement [saar-te-ne-mong]—certainly
C'est absurd [set aab-sour-dah]—that's absurd
Chaque chose en son temps [sha-kuh sho-zh ang song tang]—each thing in its own time
Coulers ici [koo-l-ers ee-see]—colors here
D'accord [duck-ohr] —agreed
Dîner [dee-neh]—dinner
Du parfum Français [du paar-fong- fraan- say]—some French perfume
Ennui [on-wee]—boredom
Excusez-moi [eh-skoo-zay mu-ah]—excuse me
Excusez-nous [eh-skoo-zay-noo]—excuse us

Fait accompli [fae-tah-come-plee]—done deal

Hâtez-vous lentement! [aat-tay-voo lawn-te-mon] –make haste but slowly

Incroyable [en-kwaa-yah-bluh]—unbelievable

Jamais [zhaa-may]—never

Je ne sais pas [zhay nay say pa]—I don't know

Je suis [zhay swee]—I am

Jouer avec des mots [zhu - eh ah-vek day moh]—play with words

La guerre [laah gai-ru]—the war

La vache [laah vaash]—oh my goodness; the literal translation is "the cow" but in French slang is means amazement

Le directeur [lo dee-rec-teur]—the director

Magnifique [maan-ee-feek]—awesome

Mais oui [ma oo-ee]—yes, of course

Manger [mawn-zhey]—to eat

Meilleurs amis pour toujours [may-ohrs aa-mees poor toozjoor]—best friends forever

Merci beaucoup [mahr-see -bo-coo]—thank you very much

Merveilleux [mehr-vay-yu]—wonderful

Mes amis [mays ah-me]—my friends

Mes chers amis [may shehrs ah-mee]—my dear friends

Mesurable [may-soo-raah-blay]—measurable

Moi [mo-ah]—me

Moi aussi [mo-ah ossee]—me too

Mon ami [mong ah-mee]—my friend

Mon cher ami [mong share ah-mee]—my dear friend

Mon meilleur ami [mong may-ohr aa-mee]—my best friend

Monsieur [mo-syeu]—mister, man

Naturellement [naa-tou-re-lle-mong]—surely

N'est-ce-pas [na-sa-pah]—don't you think

Nous mangeons [new mawn-zhong]—we eat

Oh là là! [oh laah laah]—Oh my! Oh goodness!

Oui [oo-ee]—yes

Ouf [oofe]—crazy; this word spelled backwards is "fou;" it means crazy

Parbleu [par-bluh]—my goodness, by golly
Parfum [par-foam]—perfume
Pas de trois [pah day twah]—ballet dance with three performers
Peut-être [poh-taitre]—maybe
Plus ça change, plus c'est la même chose [ploo sa shawn-zhe, ploo say la meh-m shows] — what goes around comes around
Pourquoi [poor-kwah]—why
Rien [ree-aing]—nothing
Quel cœur [kell koer]—how bold-hearted
Quel courage [kell coo-raa-zhey]—what courage
Quel domage [kell doh-maa-zhey]—what a pity
Quelle horreur [kell orr-eur]—what horror
Qu'est -ce que c'est? [kai-se-ke-ceh]—what is that
S'il vous plaît [seel voo play]—please
Spécifique [spay-see-feek]—specific
Splendide [splaan-dee-de]—splendid
Superbe [soo-per-baih]—terrific
Tête-à-tête [teht ah teht]—private conversation between two
Très bien [tray b-yan]—very good, very well
Vas-y [wa-zee]—let's go

Hawaiian

Aloha [aloha]—hello, goodbye, peace, affection, compassion, mercy

Maori

Ae—yes
Haka—traditional Maori warrior dance
Kai—food
Kia ora—hello, be well
Koha—gift
Puku—belly

New Zealand Slang (with the great vowel shift)

Ay—good
Bro—mate, dude
Choice bro—cool, okay, very good
Crisps—chips
Don't spit the dummy—don't get angry [dummy—pacifier]
Faaa—far out, as in disappointment or excitement
Good on ya, mate—well done
Hanker—feel a strong desire
Hardout—yeah
Heaps—a lot
Keen ay—good
Mare—nightmare
Mate—friend
Nay, nay—no
She'll be right mate—it will all be okay, things will be fine
Spit the dummy—throw a fit
Sweet-as bro—really good, awesome
Sweet-as stink, fella— really good
Throw a sickie—take time off
To hanker—to guess
Yeah, yeah, nah—yes and no
You alright—what's up
You are spinning yarn—you are exaggerating, lying, or telling
a long story

Epilogue

Education breeds confidence.
Confidence breeds hope.
Hope breeds peace.

Confucius (551- 479 BC)

Bibliography

Drucker, Peter F: The Practice of Management. Harper & Row Publishers, New York and Evanston 1954

Holland, Jennifer S.: Unlikely Friendships. 47 Remarkable Stories from the Animal Kingdom. Workman Publishing, New York 2011

King, Carolyn: Immigrant Killers. Introduced Predators and the Conservation of Birds in New Zealand. Oxford University Press, Auckland 1984

Michener, James A.: Return to Paradise Random House New York 1951

Owen, Alvin: How the Kiwi Lost its Wings. Illustrations by Dave Gunson. Reed Children's Books, an Imprint of Reed Publishing (NZ) Ltd., Auckland New Zealand 2002

Reed, A.W.: Reed Book of Maori Mythology. Reed Publishing (NZ) Auckland 2004

Safina, Carl: Beyond Words. What Animals Think and Feel. Henry Holt & Co., New York NY 2015

Wilson, Edward O: Biophilia. Harvard University Press, Cambridge MA 1984

Printed in the United States
By Bookmasters